Bloodlust
By Anya Clara

Trigger Warnings

The author of this book would like the reader to be aware of some of the triggers of this book. If any of these should make you uncomfortable, please consider a different story.

These triggers include (but are not limited to)
Desperately trying to meet every possible vampire trope available, characters letting out breaths they are holding, heaving bosoms and women in impractical nightwear, historical inaccuracies (don't pretend you came here for that), declarations of love (or similar) that no realistic man would ever say, men who can find a clitoris with no guidance, lots of rain- like unholy amounts of rain that should realistically cause a flood, more tropes than really necessary and characters who make bad choices and who really, really should know better but then it just wouldn't be dramatic.

But, on a more serious note - **there will be blood, non consensual sex, mind control and discussions about death and suicidal thoughts.**

This isn't quite a *dark romance*. It's more of a fuzzy gray. It's more of a 'dip your toes in the dark side' rather than a walk in the deep dark forbidden woods.

I.

Abigail sat across from her mother and nodded gravely.

"So you see, my dear, what Mr Jacobs is proposing is not only a wonderful deal for you, but also of great benefit to the family." Her mother said,

She kept her blue eyes focussed on her hands, she did not dare look up at the man sitting across from her. She didn't want to acknowledge what he was asking of her, let alone respond. Her mother continued to ramble on,

"He is from such a prestigious family, financially, you will be secure. Your future children will be secure. This is a wonderful opportunity." She could hear her mother's tone becoming more and more high pitched, desperately trying to convince her that this was the right thing to do. She could feel her own heart racing, her chest quaking.

Mr Jacobs was not her first choice for marriage. He would not even make the top ten... hundred. He was a plain and portly man, perhaps three times her own age. He was a merchant, by trade, and had heavy dealings in spices and silks coming in from the east. He was wealthy - he did have that going for him. That was about it. He was arrogant, entitled and uncaring. He had made his position on the expectations of marriage clear a long time ago. Women were baby making factories for his family dynasty, they had no rights or privileges. His last wife, Bessie Mockton, had died in labor. The babe had survived and since been sent off to a boarding school somewhere in the south. Arthur or Alban or something like that. She could vaguely remember his face, his round rosy cheeks and mop of red hair. Frederick Jacobs had shown no love for the child and the second he was of age, he was gone. Would the same be true of any children she produced? She took a long steadying breath. Her mother had just finished speaking and by now, she'd expect an answer. Abigail looked up at the man across from her.

He had beads of sweat on his forehead, the remaining hair that he had was brushed over his balding head. She felt bile rise in her throat at the idea of him kissing her, of him touching her...she swallowed it down. Her breath was shaky as she forced a coy smile.

"Thank you, Mr Jacobs for your kind offer..." She licked her lips, "I have much to think about." She could see the rage glint in her mother's eyes and the angry redness burn under Mr Jacob's skin. She stood quickly, her mind racing. "I must beg your pardon, I have errands to run-in the village." She backed away, curtsying as she did so, grabbing a shawl from a peg by the door, "I thank you again, Mr Jacobs...Mother. I will give you my answer soon." She pulled open the wooden door and shut it quickly behind her, the faint sound of her mother's voice apologizing profusely to the piggy man in their kitchen.

She thought she might vomit. She felt knotted to her stomach and sick to her core. She took a few long, deep breaths of the fresh autumn air. The trees had started to change and apples had begun to fall from the trees. How apt that her favorite time of year should become the beginning of the end for her. She felt tears well up in her eyes. She brushed them away with the back of her hand, composed herself and headed down to the market.

The village square was beautiful. Thatched roofs and stone walls, the small amber orchard trees dropped leaves into the mud roads. The smell of pine from the nearby forest could be smelled almost all year round, and the brook to the south provided a good amount of freshwater fish. Abigail had lived here her entire life. She felt as if it were a little piece of heaven, right in the heart of Europe. Up until seven years ago, she was sure she had the perfect life. It had changed, almost overnight when the English attacked. The country had gone to war. She didn't know why, nor did she care, war was the game of noblemen and kings, not the concern of lowland's villagers. But then, they started to lose. The army had come to town and signed up every young man of eligible age. Her father and two elder brothers had left. Benjamin had scarcely turned 16 when he was called up. At first, they used to write. Her father wrote that it would be all over in a few months - that neither side had the resources. Her eldest brother Jack, had written of bloody battles - and that Abigail mustn't worry - but then, the letters stopped.

All letters stopped.

No one in the village received word from the war again. And no one came back. That was five years ago. Part of her still hoped to see them come marching back into the square, battered and bruised - but alive. But it didn't happen. And with each passing season, hope began to fade.

She'd been only 13, and now, she was responsible for everything. So much had changed. Her mother, wracked with grief, was barely fit to manage the household any longer, and Abigail knew that the only way to secure their future was to wed. It was her duty, and she despised it. Every day she cursed the blasted war that had pulled her brothers away, that had taken her father. She cursed it to heaven and back for taking the soul of her mother and cursed it again for taking her freedom.

She knew she would have to say yes to Mr Jacobs. They were running out of money - like many other people and they were running out of options. They'd sold off much of the silverware and fineary that they had owned. Abigail had tried to take up employment as a nanny or as a seamstress, but with hard times falling on the entire village, employment was hard to keep. She'd hoped that a miracle would present itself by now, but none had come. She felt the bitter tears rise up in her again, for she had another matter to deal with.
And that was Daniel.

Daniel, was a stableboy in a nearby village. He visited from time to time when the market was in town.

Only a year older than her, he had been too young when the draft had come in. He'd lied about his age and tried desperately to join the other men - but the army had caught him and sent him home. He had blond wavy hair and emerald eyes. His skin always seemed to be sunkissed and he had broad shoulders and strong arms. Abigail had found herself admiring him on several occasions, and she knew that he too, admired her. They had become fast friends in the past year, and Abigail had dreamed of running away with him- of starting a new life, with no worries somewhere totally new. But, alas, it wasn't to be. Like herself, Daniel was not rich. He made enough to get by but not enough to support her mother too. Had the war not taken place, perhaps in another life, she would be his wife. But this was not that life, and she knew that today, she would need to say goodbye to him.

As she approached the village square she pulled her shawl a little tighter as she looked around. The market was bustling with trade and she smiled to herself at the people around her, going about their lives as best they could. She looked around, her eyes straining in the light - and then she saw him. He stood at the edge of the market, a strong, brown stallion reined in his hands. His brown waistcoat was open and his shirt slightly open, his strong chest visible beneath. His eyes met hers and he gave her a warm smile, beckoning her over. She felt her stomach flutter. He was everything that Frederick Jacobs was not. Kind, thoughtful and handsome. Her heart panged with sadness as she walked towards him, knowing what she had to do.

"Abby - you look beautiful this morning." She smiled, sadly.

"Daniel," she put a hand on the horse's nose, stroking softly, "How are you?"

"All the better for seeing you. I was hoping you'd be here."

"Oh?" Was all she could muster. She couldn't look him in the eyes. She knew she needed to tell him.

"Is everything alright?" His voice was laced with concern. He placed a paw-like hand on her shoulder, his comforting warmth radiating through her body. Any other time, she would have felt at ease and completely relaxed, but not today. She shook her head, blinking back tears. He turned her to face him, holding her at arms length as he surveyed her face. "What's wrong, Abs? You can tell me anything."

"I-I…" She tried to push down the emotion, the fear of everything that was to become of her life. Once she said it outloud, she knew it was all true - that the dream was over. She squeezed her eyes shut and looked away. She didn't want to see his reaction. "Mr Jacobs has asked for my hand in marriage." The words stuttered from her mouth in a clumsy cascade. She could feel herself tremble. There. She had said it. "And I am afraid that I must oblige his wishes and become his wife." Her shoulders began to shake as she sobbed. She could no longer hold it in. Daniel's grip became firmer and he pulled her into his chest. She felt his huge arms wrap around her as she buried his face into his chest. He smelled of hay and fresh air. He smelled of a home she knew she could never have. He pulled her closer, and she could hear his heart beating as he stroked her back softly.

"Do you want to marry Mr Jacobs?"

"Of course not!" She tried to push herself away, angry at the suggestion that this could even be close to what she wanted, "But what choice do I have?" Daniel frowned, his face down cast.

"Marry me." He spoke softly, and her heart raced. She had long wished to hear those words from his lips, but they both knew it wouldn't be possible.

"Daniel, you know that-"

"Why not?" He looked serious. He brushed a lock of hair from his face. "I may not have the wealth that Mr Jacobs does, but I can provide for you. Come back with me, to my village. We can live there - together…" She took his hand in her own. How she wished this was possible,

"But what about my mother, Daniel? She is a widow. She has no income. Who will provide for her?"

"I will work more hours. We can move to a town or a city- Abby- I will earn enough if I can keep you. We will send the money back to her." He clasped her hands in his. "I promise, we can make this work. Please- tell me you will consider this, seriously, before you give Mr Jacobs your answer?" He looked imploringly at her. He was serious. It was a childish dream but her heart leapt at the option.

"Why have you only asked me now, Daniel?" She

needed to know the answer. She knew that she loved him and that he admired her, but he'd never been so bold. She had dreamed of being his wife and he had never before asked.

"I did not know your situation was so immediate. Abby-" She smiled, softly, letting go of his hand. "Please - before you give your answer to Mr Jacobs - think of me as a serious offer. Consider me a viable option and I will strive to make this work. I want you to be happy - Abigail. I may not have the wealth that Mr Jacobs has, and the life I can offer you, will not be as comfortable, but do not disregard my proposal, for it is earnest and of good intent." He took a step back, his eyes glittering. Abigail could feel the fluttering in her stomach return, her heart pounding in her chest. "I do not need your answer now - but please, whatever your answer may be, please give it to me yourself."

"I will." She took a step back, breathless. Her mind was racing. She could no longer think of the tasks she had come to do as she felt her thoughts spiral out of control. Was this possible? Could she marry Daniel? Was she dreaming and would she wake up from a feverish dream in the arms of Frederick Jacobs? She shook her head. No. She needed to get out - to clear her head.

She nodded, dazed and overwhelmed as she wandered back to her home. She let herself in and went straight to her little room, ignoring the shouts from her mother and she sat on her bed, thinking.
She didn't know how long she had sat there, but the bright blue sky had faded to lilac and then to red.

The sun hung low in the sky. She felt as though she was finally settled in her thoughts when a gentle knock came at the door. Her mother pushed it open and handed her a small envelope. She didn't speak but handed it over silently. Abigail took it and turned it over in her hands.

"Abigail, I think it is very important that you respond to Mr Jacobs. He has been very kind in extending this offer to you, lord knows we are not the most fortunate people in the village and-"

"I know, mother." Abigail ran her fingers along the paper, as her mother perched on the edge of the bed.

"I know this is not what you expected in life. I expect you feel overwhelmed, but we cannot risk this opportunity."

"Yes, mother."

"I am expecting him to call again at breakfast tomorrow. He will want your answer. Abigail. Do the right thing." With that, her mother stood up and left.

The right thing. Right for her mother. Possibly right for her. There was no love from Mr Jacobs. He just wanted a pretty young bride and Abigail met that criteria. Plenty of years of child rearing left in her. Would she be broken and worn in like Bessie had been? Apparently Bessie had been a willful and rebellious young woman before marriage. After that, she was quiet and demure - old Mrs Bailey said she hardly recognized her. Is that what would happen? Abigail thought of her mother. Her graying hair and aging face. She was perhaps still younger than Mr Jacobs herself, though it was impolite to ask. Would her mother be able to marry Jacobs? Abby laughed at the thought. Her mother had passed the age of childbearing and the poor woman had lost a husband and two sons. She had endured enough.

Was Daniel really an option? Was it just crazy dreams? She looked down at the letter in her hands. She had almost forgotten it was there. She opened it slowly and recognised the familiar scrawl of Daniel's pen-

'My sweet Abigail,
I have long thought of asking you to be my bride but have never found the courage to speak the words in my heart. I cannot bear the thought of losing you to another. I look forward to our every meeting, and have done since the moment I laid eyes on you. You have always been the most beautiful woman I know, and the cleverest I should ever hope to meet. I could watch the sunlight sparkle in your golden hair for hours, and listen to the wonderful nothings that you speak when we are together. The mere thought of never again sharing a moment with you is too much to consider. I am sorry that my proposal has come so late, but I have realized that I must speak my truth to you now, or accept that it will be forever my own burden to bear. Abigail James, I love you. I have loved you since the day we met and have fought with emotion ever since. I love

you so wholly and incredibly that I can no longer contain these thoughts as my own. I must share them with you, I must declare my unyielding love for you in hope that we can be together. I cannot offer you riches, but I will spend the rest of my days working to make you happy, working to bring light into your life as you do for me. I can find employment in the city. Let us run away together, tonight, and start anew. We shall send money back to your mother, as promised, and we shall live a humble life. You deserve the world, and I am sorry that I cannot give it to you, but I can give you myself and my promise.

I will be in the forest clearing tonight, beside the rocks and lake. If you do not come, I will know your decision and shall not pursue you again. I shall wait all night if I need to.

I love you,
With all of my hope,
Daniel.'

She read the letter over again, and over again. Her heart was racing. She had to do it. She knew, in that moment, that she would regret it the rest of her life if she did not try. If she did not take this chance with the man she loved. She scrambled to her drawer and pulled out a piece of paper and dipped her quill in ink. She would leave a note for her mother. She knew this would break her heart - but she would invite her back to the city in a few months' time, once they were settled. The village was their home, but it needn't be their tomb. She had prayed for a miracle and now that she had one, she had to take it. How could she have ever considered otherwise?

She scribbled the letter down hastily before signing it. Her heart was pounding in her chest. She needed to leave soon, before she could reconsider - or else she may never leave at all. Sweet Daniel - he would become her savior.

She layered up her clothes, placed the letter neatly on her pillow, and then crept down the stairs. She closed the door gently behind her before running towards the forest as the silvery moon rose high into the night sky.

II.

By the time Abigail arrived at the forest the sky had blackened. The moon cast little useful light and the flamelight from the village was far away. She stumbled over fallen branches and twigs as she searched for the clearing. As she clambered deeper into the trees she found herself thinking of her new life with Daniel, the possibilities it would bring. She felt warm in the cool autumn breeze at the thought of spending her days with him. Before she knew it, the village was completely out of sight, and the edge of the trees was nowhere to be seen. She listened out for the calming sound of the river, but she could not hear it.

She felt her heart pound as she felt around, the darkness snaring in. The woods were not the same place by night as they were by day. She could feel herself growing weary as the slithers of shimmering light faded and shadows cast over the only light. She was in total darkness.

Her blood felt cold as she could hear the crack of twigs, each rustle of leaves. It was ill-advised to go into the forest at night, she knew this. Of course she had heard the tales of monsters as a child, but now fully grown - what could hurt her? They were fairy stories, surely? With each frightful snap and susurration of leaves she found herself less and less sure. She continued to roam deeper - perhaps this had been a bad idea - perhaps they should have waited until dawn...

After what felt like hours of walking, Abigail knew she was completely lost. She knew she needed to turn back, but every direction was the same. There was no way to tell where she had come from, and where she was going. She called out Daniel's name over and over, but no reply came. How had this happened? How had she gotten so off course? She continued to walk forwards, at least at some point the woods would end and she'd be able to find a village or town nearby? But what of Daniel? Would he think her answer was no? That she had chosen Mr Jacobs and his money in the end? The thought was unbearable. She had come for him - she had intended to be his bride, but it had all gone so horribly wrong.

She called out again, and again. There was no answer, the only sound was that of the forest - it was hopeless. She found a fallen tree and sat upon it, fighting off the urge to sob. Should she sleep here tonight? Was it safe? She'd walked for hours and dawn must be close, it had to be, but the foliage was so dense that no light could penetrate through.

She began to sob. Perhaps this was her punishment for being selfish, for wanting something other than her duty? What would she tell her mother and Mr Jacobs? She'd been foolish. Poor Daniel - he was probably sitting alone by the rocks in the clearing - waiting for her. She closed her eyes- she could picture him there now.

It was oddly clear. He was waiting with a gray horse, the river bubbling peacefully, the moonbeams illuminating his skin. He was hopeful and calm. He looked undeterred. In her mind, she saw him turn to the noise of a crack -

"Abigail - I thought that-"

"No, foolish boy."...Mr Jacobs? Abby tried to open her eyes but found herself surrounded by the strange dream. She turned to see the trees surrounding the clearing. She was there with them - she called out - they did not turn. They could not see her, nor could they hear her voice.

"Mr Jacobs, what are you doing here?"

"I have come to make you an offer." The large man sidled up to Daniel. He reached the blond man's shoulders but carried himself as many powerful men do. Daniel did not falter,

"Thank you, Mr Jacobs, but I have no business with you today."

"Now now boy - do not be deterred too easily. This opportunity will make you rich. It will make you wealthier than you could ever dream. Perhaps enough to look after a bride…" He grinned a wicked grin. Daniel swallowed and tilted his head, his curiosity peaked. Abigail called out again - *no, do not listen to him,* she shouted her voice sore and fading - but it was no use. "I have some merchant ships arriving at the coastlands in a few days. My back isn't what it was and I'd appreciate a younger man on this journey. Now, since the war, there have been bandits, or something, on the path. A few of my recent...employees...have vanished. But-" He came in closer to the man, speaking conspiratorially, "None of them were as strong as you, as big as you. You're a clever man Daniel. You're quick. I've seen you chase down and harness wild horses. I will pay you handsomely for your quest. Say, six hundred pieces." He cocked an eyebrow. Abigail gasped. 600 pieces? That was a ludicrous amount - it would pay off her mother's rent for forty years - it was the kind of money only lords had...it was too good to be real.

"Thank you, Mr Jabobs, that is a kind offer, but I promised I would wait-"

"Do not worry yourself about that." He waved his hand, "I will pass on the message, *of course.* I'm sure dear Abigail will wait for you, and she will understand." Daniel opened his mouth to speak and then closed it again. "I saw the letter, boy. But I am a fair man. I am giving you this *option,* but do not be naive. You will take up my employment, and you will leave town to do this. I will pay you, *if* you return. But this silly game is over."

"I will not." Daniel drew himself up to his full height, he towered over the portly man, "I will wait here, for Abigail."

"She will not come. I have seen to that." Abigail shook her head - he was lying. Of course she was coming, she stood up and ran towards them, but the image of them did not come closer.

"What have you done to her, Frederick?" Anger laced Daniel's voice, his fist were clenched tightly. Mr Jacobs laughed mirthlessly,

"Nothing...yet. But, if you know what is good

for you, and more importantly, good for *her,* you will take this generous offer. I will not make it again." His piggy eyes watched Daniel, a thin lipped smile crossing his face as the taller man sagged. "Good man." He patted him on the back, handing him a slip. "Go here. Give them this. I will tell Abigail of your employment. She will be safe." He laughed, wickedly. Daniel shook his head, climbing upon the steed. He kicked it firmly before pulling away and galloping out of the clearing. Abby watched helplessly as Mr Jabobs took up Daniel's position in the clearing, a satisfied smirk on his face. She knew that whilst Daniel could easily overpower the man, he would not be victorious for long. Mr Jacobs was in favor in the country courts, he knew *people* and Daniel would just as well disappear if Frederick wished it.

She looked around in cold confusion as the image faded as a swarm of bats raced above her head, swooping towards the sky. Her heart pounded at the sudden shock and rush of air as they passed her. They were gone within a moment and she found herself alone again. The log she had previously sat upon was gone. In her confusion, she continued to wander. It was a miracle she hadn't fallen or bumped into a tree. She was cold and frightened now and everything felt hopeless. Had the vision been real? Was it just her terror playing tricks on her? If she reached the clearing - would Jacobs be there instead of Daniel? She dried her eyes - she needed to move forward - she couldn't stay in this god forsaken place any longer.

A loud, ear piercing crack cut through the

sky and the darkness illuminated. Seconds later an almighty downpour fell from the heavens, drenching her completely. It was the last thing she needed. She was cold, she was angry and she was so confused. What was even real anymore?

She began to run, searching for a cave or something to take shelter in - she'd seen enough thunderstorms to know that trees were beacons for lightning.

So she ran, stumbling and soaking, her hair twisting and sticking to her face, her skirts muddy and heavy.

Then she saw it. A clearing in the dense trees. A hilltop, and upon it a large, looming castle. Lightning sliced the sky around it, the rain poured. She had never seen it before, and yet, it looked...inviting. It would be safe there. She could feel herself drawn towards it. She wrapped the shawls closer, trying to cover her head as best she could. She hoped the family who lived there would be kind and let her take shelter.

She was out of breath, her chest heaving as she finally reached the large oak doors. She looked around. The trees surrounding the castle were dead, burnt or broken. She could see a sheer drop where perhaps a moat had once been - but, no, she shook her head, it was far too deep. It was like a ravine all around her, save the path she had come in on. It was a defensive structure - and yet, it towered over the forest, oppressing everything with its shadow. How had she never seen it before? Was she really so far from the village? She reached out a trembling hand to knock at the door-

It opened before she could touch it. It creaked

ominously, the sound echoing into the vestibule. She looked around, expecting to hear a servant or see a maid. There was no one. A boom of thunder startled her and she stepped inside - the door slamming shut behind her. She turned quickly - but it was too late. She was inside, and from her first glance around - she appeared to be alone.

III.

She took a few cautious steps forward, each one echoing on the flagstones.

"Hello?" She called. "Someone opened the door but-" She peered around, "but I can't seem to find them." Her heart was pounding. Something felt wrong. She couldn't put her finger on it. She pulled her wet clothes closer as she walked further into the entrance room, a cold chill in the air. Perhaps it had been warmer outside in the rain...

She turned back to the door. Perhaps the wind had blown in open...and closed. Perhaps she hadn't been invited in at all. The place didn't feel hospitable and so she turned on her heel and headed back to the door. She pulled at the handle. It did not budge. The door did not move. She pulled again. Her heart began to pound, her blood racing through her veins. A bat swooped by from an old arrow slit, casting an oddly large shadow as it did so. She pushed herself back against the door.

"I'm really sorry-" She called out, "I thought someone had opened the door. I see that may not have been the case..." She looked around, keeping herself firmly against the oak - ready to escape. The place was silent, "Hello?"

"Madame." She almost jumped out of her skin. An old, wrinkled man stood beside her. She suppressed a scream. She had not seen him approach. His footsteps were silent,

"I'm sorry I-"

"Please. Follow me." He spoke in long droll tones and without waiting for her response, began to walk away from the foyer. She looked around desperately - what else could she do? So, she followed him. He walked slowly, for someone who had appeared so quickly. He walked soundlessly and wordlessly through into a reception room where he gestured to a wooden chair. Abigail sat down and watched as the old man began to build a fire.

"Oh, I can help-" He shook his head.

"Please, remain here. This is my job. The master has instructed me to make you…comfortable."

"Your…master?" She raised an eyebrow.

"Yes, Madame." The fireplace roared to life, the gentle sizzle of the flames masking the sound of the heavy rain. Abigail felt her mind race. Who was the master of this castle? She wasn't sure where she was, let alone who the nobility of the area might be.

"I apologize for my ignorance, sir, but I am afraid I lost my way in the woods. I am not sure where I am, or who your master might be. I do not want to offend him, might I know his name?" The old man's face was impassive.

"Indeed." Abigail leaned forward, but the man said nothing further and his face was impassive. Indeed? What the hell did that mean? She could feel herself growing angry. It had been a long night and a difficult day. She felt as though she was reaching the end of her patience. She took a steady breath.

"Would you be so kind as to tell me the family who keeps this..." She looked around, "charming estate, please?"

"Not a family, Madame. Just the Master. He lives here, alone. Save for myself, of course." Still no answers. She opened her mouth to speak again but the man had vanished. She looked around...he had been there but a moment ago. She was tired. She knew this. She must have missed him leaving. She took a moment to take in her surroundings.

The fireplace was huge, by far the most prominent feature of the room. The stone bricks entombed the rest of the space with two, large tapestries hanging on opposite walls. Above the fireplace hung 3 shields, the newest perhaps 10 years old, the eldest....Abigail was unsure, but it looked ancient. She noticed a few sets of armor adorning the doorway, large pikes in the hands. A huge, metal chandelier hung from the ceiling but it remained unlit, the only light was cast from the fire. The reception room, like the foyer, had a strange chill in the air, but the fire fought to change that. A warm glow seeped from it, lighting the dark red rug that covered the dusty flagstones.

Just the Master? She pondered on this. The castle was ancient, hundreds of years old. The family had to be ancient too, she supposed. She was certain she hadn't crossed the county's border - but she had never been to the capital. The castle wasn't this old though...was it? She tried to think about everything she had learned. No...castles were...defensive...strategic. Given to lords for battle honors and vallour in the olden times - now their heirs and families ran them. They paid heavy taxes to the King in the capital. The capital was a city - cities were bigger than villages... so this couldn't be the capital. She hadn't seen any other houses or buildings on the approach.

A defensive building. It had the ravine. The sheer approach. What did this place defend? Did the surrounding area still exist?

She shook her head. None of it mattered. The storm outside pounded against the stained windows. At least she was out of the storm and the Master...whoever he may be, was kind enough to let her in for the night.

"A drink, Madame." The old man appeared beside her again. Startled, she drew back. She wished he wouldn't do that. He presented her with a glass of red wine. She took it cautiously.

"Thank you." She placed it to her lips,

"Madame may prefer to remove her wet clothing. I shall have it cleaned...and dried." His dull tones drew each word out.

"I am afraid I have nothing to change into. I cannot be in your Master's home dressed...indecently." The man stared at her though emotionless eyes. He took a deep sigh.

"If you wish to remove the outermost layers, Madame." He turned away. With his back to her, she looked around...right here? Right now? She did have several layers on...she'd dressed to run away. She stood and slowly began to peel the sodden layers off. Two skirts, three blouses and a cloak were removed, and folded, with a slosh, before being handed over to the old man. He turned around and nodded gravely before taking the clothes and walking away.

She sat back into the wooden chair. She was left in her white nightdress, covered by a simple dress and blouse. It was damp, but nowhere near as wet as the garments she had already removed. She took a small sip from the glass. The wine was musty and spicy. It had rich, heavy tones - this was not something the local tavern served. She savored another sip, closing her eyes. She could feel the warm fire on her now, warming her through the clothes. She took another sip - it felt so wonderful. So calming. She felt herself relax... becoming oddly at ease.

Another sip. It was deliciously moreish. She could feel her mind loosening. The fire warming her skin. Perhaps...perhaps it would feel warmer still without her blouse. She placed the glass down, in a trance like state, unfastening the laces at the front of her dress. She slipped the sleeves over her shoulders and down her arms. Her dress, now hanging around her waist, the fire's warmth now even more delightful on her skin...she began to unfasten her blouse. She pulled loose the strings before pulling it slowly over her head. She could feel the flames heating her cold skin... the unyielding, healing warmth. Her head felt light and dazed as she let the dress fall to her feet as she stepped out of it, walking closer to the fire.

She could hear the roar of the storm- but it felt so far away…but the crackle of the fire…that was close. She pulled off her boots and peeled down her stockings… the carpet plush under her cold toes. As if she were dreaming she picked up the wine, and sipped again as she walked closer to the fire, now, only in her thin, white nightdress. She loosened the buttons, exposing the top of her chest, allowing the warmth to lick at it, to warm the blood that coursed through her veins.

A part of her realized what she was doing - how exposed, how indecent she was in the strangers home- but she took another long sip of the wine and the thoughts melted away.

"Yes…" She heard the voice in her head, "Let go for me…" The voice was soothing, like a lullaby. She closed her eyes, letting the heat wash over her, the aroma of the wine encapsulating her. She felt unsteady and began to sway slightly on her feet. She let her head fall back, her body drinking in the warmth. She could feel her heart rushing, the voice called out in her mind again, "Relinquish your control to me…" It was hypnotizing, alluring. She placed the glass to her lips again-

"Madame." The cool tones of the old man cut through the haze. Abigail blinked back to her senses. She turned quickly, realizing what she was doing. She looked down at herself. The top of her bosom was exposed, she was showing a scandalous amount of cleavage. She pulled her nightdress closed, her cheeks burning with embarrassment.

"I am so sorry. I apologize. I do not know what came over me, I-" She wanted to tell him that she was not this sort of woman, that she knew better, but the old man cut her off.

"A room has been prepared for you. Please, follow me." She hurried to collect her things, placing her wine on the mantle as she did so.

She gripped her damp clothes close to her body as she followed the old man back to the foyer and up the cold stone steps. She felt humiliated. What had come over her? She'd been standing in the reception room of a nobleman, swaying in her nightgown like some sort of harlot. She felt sick to her stomach. Was this the type of woman she was? The kind who turned down the proposal of a wealthy man, to run away with a stableboy and then dance naked in the home of a nobleman? Her father would be so ashamed if he knew. She shook her head, pushing the thoughts away. It had been a difficult day, and a more difficult night.

She followed the old man through the cool, dark corridors before reaching an open door. He bid her inside.

"This will be your room." She took a few steps inside. An ornate four-poster bed stood in the center of the room, adorned with thick red and gold curtains and velvet bedsheets. An ebony closet and writing desk stood against another wall, and a small table besides the bed, with a single burning candle next to it. The window was open. The heavy velvet curtains did not move, but the lighter curtain liner blew dramatically into the room. She turned to thank the man, but he had already disappeared, the door clicking shut as he did so.

She immediately turned and pulled at the door. At this point, she was unsurprised, but still alarmed, to find that it was locked.

IV.

Abigail felt that she should be panicking, that being locked in the room should frighten her. She took a moment to ponder the situation - she had been given wine. The room had a nice bed. She was not in the storm. Overall, things could be worse. She wandered across to the flapping curtains and pulled the window closed. There was little else to do other than sleep. She pulled down the sheets and crawled in. The mattress was soft and inviting and for the time being, she felt safe. Tomorrow, she would leave the castle, and look for a way home. She would find Daniel and apologize, she'd speak to her mother and Mr Jacobs and fix everything. But now, the beginning of dawn was creeping through the window, and she desperately needed to sleep.

Sleep came easily to her but her dreams were odd. She dreamt of running down the castle's hallways, her nightgown billowing behind her pursued by an unknown assailant. It was exhilarating - she was enjoying the chase but somehow felt like prey...such an odd sensation. She would hide behind pillars, flee downstairs, but all the while - she found that she was almost *hoping* to be caught. She glanced over her shoulder - she could not see the chaser. Everytime she looked, her heart would race and she found herself wishing to be...ravished? It caught her off guard - she could feel the desire for someone to be holding her close, kissing up her body, kissing her neck as she leaned back, the stone wall against her back. She could not see the man in her dreams - he was hazy...but the desire for him was growing. Who was the mystery man? She let her dreams take over, as the stranger ran his hands over her flesh, unfastening her nightdress, exposing her shoulders - her breasts. Her head lolling backwards as she exposed her neck, her blond curls pushed aside as he licked and kissed and...bit.

She woke up with a start in the bed, her face clammy, her heart racing. She looked around, she was alone in the room. She looked down to find her night dress unfastened, her shoulders and breasts exposed. Her heart pounded. It was a dream. It had been a dream. She reassured herself. Shakily, she walked across to the window. Sunlight filled the sky, it was late into the morning and the sun was climbing towards the center of the sky. Abigail climbed out of bed, letting her feet touch the dark wooden floors. She looked around. Her clothes were neatly piled on the writing desk across the room. When did they come back? She couldn't remember anyone entering her room. A moment of panic washed over her as she remembered her dream. She found herself praying that she hadn't muttered or mumbled, and that her nightgown was still fastened when her clothes were returned.

She was pleased to find a small washbasin next to the clothing. She took the cloth and washed her face and body, scrubbing away the dirt from the forest. She was pleased to find the water was still a little warm. She pulled her clothes back on, choosing not to layer everything. She'd carry them home instead, that way, if she was caught in the rain, she would at least have a dry-ish option.

She pulled at the bedroom door and found that it swung open. Had it even been locked? She had been tired and confused last night. She probably dreamt the whole thing. She looked up and down the long hallways, trying to remember the way to the foyer.

The corridor was dimly lit, very little natural light penetrated them, and small candelabras were positioned for a modest amount of illumination. The castle felt ancient. It was well kept, but the decor and furniture had scarcely been updated in perhaps two... maybe three hundred years.

"Madame." The voice made her jump.

"Oh, hello, I was-"

"If you would kindly follow me, a breakfast has been prepared."

"Oh I-" She had planned to say she did not need to eat, she needed to leave to find Daniel and get back to the village, but the old man had already begun to walk away. She hurried a little to catch up. "Thank you for your hospitality, but I need to leave-"

"That will not be possible." The even tone cut her off, "The Master insisted that a meal was prepared."

"Thank you...er..I'm sorry, I never caught your name-erm-"

"I did not give it to you." Well, that was that.

"Oh, er-" She tried to rally,

"Breakfast has been served. The Master insists that you eat."

"Will your Master be present?"

"I am afraid that is not possible." There was no hint of emotion in his voice. He led her to the dining room where a long banquet table was set, dishes on silverware at the head seat.

The table was ridiculously long. Abigail surveyed it. No one, not even a lord, could know enough people to sit at this table. It was obscene. The man pulled out a chair for her and nodded for her to sit. She did not feel much like eating, and she really did need to leave, but the host had been so generous, it would be rude not to oblige. She sat down and glanced at the old man, who pulled the lids from several dishes. She looked at the cooked meat and fruits. There was far too much for one person, it was overwhelming.

"Will other people be joining me?" She asked hopefully.

"No Madame."

"I am afraid I cannot eat all of this food. It looks delicious though, thank you." She carefully picked up an apple, placed it on her plate and sliced it. She placed a segment in her mouth. It was juicy and perfectly ripe.

"You said your Master will not be joining me?"

"That is correct, Madame."

"May I have the chance to meet him before I depart?"

"I am afraid that will not be possible."

"Oh, I am sorry." She took another segment,

"Does he have duties to attend? I should like to thank him, and yourself, for the kindness you have shown me."

"He sleeps during the day, Madame."

"Oh." Was all she could muster. She could not remember seeing him last night. Perhaps he was busy attending to his affairs. How strange. She finished the apple in silence, took a sip from the goblet of water and then stood. She looked for the old man, who had disappeared, yet again.

"Madame." He appeared beside her. Surely he was not there a moment ago. What a strange man.

"Oh, hello. I was wondering if you had some paper, and perhaps some ink, so that I may write a note to thank your Master?"

"That will not be necessary, Madame."

"Oh. I shall collect my things and prepare to take my leave. Thank you, again, for your hospitality."

"That shall not be necessary."

"I beg your pardon?"

"To collect your things."

"Oh, but they are in the bed chamber."

"Yes, Madame."

"I should like to take them with me."

"Where to, Madame?"

"Home, of course. I wonder if you could point me in the direction of-"

"That will not be possible, Madame."

"I'm sorry?"

"To leave." She was taken aback. Whatever did he mean?

"Why not?"

"The storm." She remembered looking out of the window that morning. The sky had been a beautiful blue - the sun was shining, there was no storm.

"What storm?" She heard a loud crack of thunder echo in the halls.

"That storm." The man's face held no humor. Abigail felt uneasy at the timing of the weather. Was this man some sort of magician? No. It was mere coincidence. It had to be. She looked around the room. Well, now what? She was stuck here for at least another few hours. How would she pass the time? The old man stood across from her. "Would Madame care to entertain herself in the library, or perhaps the drawing room?" She nodded, dumbly. Why not? The man shuffled away and obediently, Abigail followed.

"You mentioned that your Master sleeps through the daytime?" She asked hopefully.

"Yes, Madame."

"Does he have work duties during the night?"

"Something like that, Madame."

"Oh. That's very unusual. Have you worked for your Master a long time?"

"All of my life, Madame." Must be a very frail old man, she found herself thinking.

"That's very impressive. You are very dutiful." He did not respond. "You mentioned that he lives alone?"

"That is correct, Madame."

"Does his family visit regularly?"

"He has no family, Madame." She felt a pang of

sadness. The thought of the two older men living alone in the castle was heartbreaking. She wondered if he had sons or grandsons lost to the war. She could not bring herself to ask.

"I'm so sorry." She walked behind him in silence, unsure of what to say next.

V.

The library was located in one of the castle's main turrets. Small arrow slits were scattered about the upper floors, a winding stone staircase providing access. The room was not particularly cozy or warm. There were long, tall bookshelves around the first floor and a table in the center. There were two wooden armchairs to one side. A few maps were on the table. She walked closer, curious to see what may be marked.

The map was large and sprawling and showed not only her country, but several neighboring ones. The main trade routes were clearly marked, as well as small metal flags.

"Is…Is this where the English are?" She asked, but no reply came. The old man had left. She ran her fingers gently over the parchment. Silver and copper flags - she was sure that's what they meant. It would make sense for a lord to know. They usually had constituents, people to send to war. Of course he would need to know how close the enemy was - how many were in their ranks. She saw the copper flags laid down near the mountains, close to the sea and the borders. Her heart sank. Were these battles lost? Were they losing? She took a step backwards. She did not need to know. She reminded herself that these were merely guesses - that she didn't know what the colors represented, that the information could easily be out of date. She glanced again at the little pewter horses along the trade routes. Whoever the Master of the castle was, was clearly involved in the running of the country. There were so many things plotted. She supposed it was normal. How else could someone be involved in government?

She tore herself away, realizing that the little map was raising her heart rate and peaking her anxiety.

She turned to the books. Many were thick, leatherbound histories and land surveys. Records of people in the area going hundreds of years back in time. A few were on war time etiquette and strategic planning. No easy reading there then. She continued to walk along the shelves, the leather binding becoming older and frayed. She looked down and the lower shelves, in hope of some fiction or something, anything, that wasn't frightfully dull. After searching, she came across a few translations of old plays. She pulled the small book out and dusted it off. It was thick with grime. She used her sleeve, the particles hung in the air for a moment, making her cough. She headed over the chair, far away from the dust cloud and opened the book. It would have to do. She huddled herself into the wooden chair and opened up the book. She could hear the storm raging outside, and she urged it to end quickly. She thought again of poor Daniel and her mother - that she had, by all accounts, disappeared without a trace. How worried they must be. She felt her heart ache with guilt. This whole endeavor had been ridiculous. She'd spend the rest of her life making it up to them.

Abby was half way through the second play when the old man's voice appeared by her ear. She had almost expected it this time.

"Madame. Dinner will be served shortly." She tried to focus on the little light coming through into the room - there was none. The thunder continued to roll outside.

"Oh," She said sadly, "Thank you." She had hoped to be away by nightfall - but she was clearly out of luck.

"Madame." He gestured for her to follow. She placed the book down gently on the chair and followed him once more.

The dining room was lit in warm light, and the fireplace, unlit at breakfast, was now roaring. Food was presented at one side, much like breakfast. The chair was pulled out for her. She took her seat, and waited politely for the food to be unveiled. There was a pause and she looked up to the old man. His face was as impassive as ever. He poured a cup of wine from the jug and unveiled the food. She took a small amount and began to slice the meat on her plate.

"Will I be dining alone again?"

"Madame." The lack of answer was expected, but it was beginning to grow tiresome. She smiled to herself, exasperated, aware that nothing she would say would bring forth more information. She ate the food and thanked the old man and by extension, the benevolent Master that she had yet to meet. It was nightfall and she began to wonder if he even existed at all. Surely he must be waking soon, and would have duties to attend to? She sighed. She would need to spend another night here, and another night without Daniel or her mother knowing where she was. She pinched the bridge of her nose,

"I am sorry to ask this, but may I spend another night?"

"Madame." The man nodded.

"I will retire, if that is acceptable." He bowed away, leaving her alone in the dining room. She sat for a few moments, drumming her fingers on the table, thinking what she should do next. She needed to leave, but what if the storm continued tomorrow? Or the day after? She could not remain here indefinitely.

She stood up from the table and headed to the bed chamber. Her clothes were still there, as she had left them this morning. She closed the door and firmed the latch, before removing her outer clothes. She ran her fingers through her hair, untangling it. She climbed into the bed and pulled the sheets over herself.

Sleep, unlike last night, did not come easy. She tossed and turned with unease thought and worry, her mind totally unsettled. She could hear the rain hammering against the window, it was loud and distracting. She pulled herself from the bed and over to the window. Without thinking, she pulled the window open, the wind and rain hitting her straight on. It felt refreshing. She could feel it against her, washing away the stress, the anxieties of what would happen next.

"*More…*" A voice whispered in her mind. *Yes.* Her inner voice responded and before she knew it, she was padding down the corridor and climbing the stairs in the turret. The flagstones were icy cold on her feet and she could hear the rain and wind howling outside. She reached the door that would lead to the battlements. She found it unlocked and as she unlatched it, the force of the gale blew it open.

She stepped outside. The wind whipped her hair and blew about her nightdress, which the rain drenched, clinging it to her body. What was she doing? She found a voice in the back of her mind fighting against her, telling her to go back inside, back into the warm. Why should she be outside, on top of a castle in a storm? But she shut it down. There was something alluring about the battlement, the rain soaking her through, the cold breeze dancing around her - it felt so…alive. It called to her. To the very core of her soul. It lit her up inside and drew her further from the door and the warmth. She looked out across the forest, the flickering of villages blinking in the darkness. She could see the merest twinkle of stars high in the sky and the moon, hidden - its position betrayed only by the soft glow that framed the clouds. She closed her eyes, the water pounding against her skin, she felt breathless at the incredible sight - she had never been so high up. She took deep steady breaths, her clothing clinging to every inch of her figure, wrapped around her thighs and bottom, her erect nipples visible through the soaked nightdress, her chest rising and falling with each intake of air. She didn't care. She was alone in the moonlight, alone with the elements, and for a moment she felt free. She spread her arms out, opening herself up to the weather, letting it drench her entirely. She knew that she should feel cold, freezing even - but the sensation was detached and far away. She felt nothing other than peace, completely at ease with herself in the pale midnight light. She opened her hazy eyes, the dreamlight state washing over her, and then, for the first time, she saw him.

A pale figure stood at the other end of the battlement. A tall, slender figure with broad shoulders. Their dark hair was soaked and pushed back. She could make out a clinging shirt and long tailcoat, flapping in the wind. That was all she could make out in the darkness. She was, once again, alarmed. How long had he been there? She was sure she had been alone when she climbed up here. She had half expected to see the little old man, but, this was certainly not him.

The spell of the weather and her trance-like state was broken by the strangers presence, and she stumbled, slipped and lost her footing from beneath her. Her heart stopped in her chest and her blood turned to ice as she discovered in a gut-wrenching moment that she had in fact been standing on the edge of the wall, and to her horror, found that she was falling - hurtling towards the endless ravine that surrounded the castle.

VI.

Abigail blinked her eyes open, the last thing she could remember was the whoosh of air rushing past her as she plummeted towards the gorge surrounding the castle. Was she dead? Her vision came into focus - no… she was inside the castle. She could hear the fireplace crackling in the hearth and the rain beating outside. She was in a bed…was it just a frightful nightmare? She placed her hands to her head - her hair was soaked. She bolted upright - this wasn't the room she had fallen asleep in. Panicked, she began to hyperventilate, she was absolutely soaking wet through, her nightdress removed, naked, in a strange bed.

"Calm down. You're fine." The voice came from across the room. Her eyes darted to the sound source. Sitting reclined in the desk chair was a slender man with broad shoulders. His hair was damp and messy, with strands falling about his pale, but handsome face. He looked as if he'd never seen sunlight. His long fingers were playing with a knife, twisting it and twirling it like a toy. He had youthful, angular features and a strong jaw with broad shoulders. He looked lazily towards her, snorting as she pulled the sheets up to cover herself and preserve what little dignity she had left. She fumbled desperately for words,

"Who are you?" Was the first thing she could think of. It was so stupid - a million other questions raced through her head, "Where am I?" He tilted his head and spoke in low, almost bored sounding tones,

"You're welcome, by the way."

"For what?" She snapped back, pulling the sheets higher, all the way up to her neck.

"I saved you." The memory of the rushing wind flooded through her head again.

"Oh..." She looked down, feeling a pang of remorse. "Thank you." He nodded, placing the knife on the table.

"The same couldn't be said for your nightgown." She looked down at the white garment in horror.

"What?" She stuttered,

"It was stuck to you, you'd have caught a fever. I needed to remove it quickly." Her eyes widened.

"You removed my nightgown?" The words were laced with anger. Who the hell did he think he was? Removing a woman's clothes was the height of indecency. No decent man would do such a thing. He may call for a maid or a handmaiden...but to do it himself was ludicrous. He simply shrugged. Abigail felt a blazing rage overtake her. How dare he. "How dare you!?" She shouted. The man was taken aback, he smiled playfully,

"How dare I? Would you have rather me let you catch a fever and die?" He spoke in a gentle English accent. Why was there an Englishman in the castle? A prisoner perhaps? The matter would have to wait.

"Yes!" She retorted, "What indecent gentleman

would remove the clothes of a woman who is not his wife?" She pulled the sheets up higher. They were not near her chin. She could feel the anger burning under her cheek. The last few days had taken their toll, and now…this.

"I am no gentleman. But duly noted. Next time, I'll let you die."

"Next time? There isn't going to be a next time. Where are my clothes? I want to leave this place right now."

"Go ahead." He gestured to the door, leaning back in the chair, "Your clothing is across the castle." Her jaw dropped. Surely he was not suggesting that she retrieve it herself? What kind of sick person was he?

"As you very well know, I cannot do that?"

"And why not?" He smirked, raising an eyebrow.

"Sir, if you even deserve that title, I am naked. I cannot very well stride naked across a stranger's castle. The mere suggestion of it-" she scoffed incredulously.

"I don't see why not." He smiled, wickedly, "Afterall, I already know what is under those sheets."

"Sir!" She scowled at him, "That is a fact that I vehemently resent. I had no control over that situation but I intend to ensure it does not happen again." She looked around the room, "Besides, among the many other reasons of which I am sure you do not need me to lay out for you, I have not yet met the Master of this estate and I would hate for him to think me indecent."

"Perhaps he likes indecent young women." The man laughed.

"Sir!"

"I will not walk naked down these halls." She watched as he stood up and took a few steps closer. She pulled back into the bed, drawing herself away from him. He stood a foot or so away from the bed,

"Are you *sure* about that?" There was a strange edge to his voice, something melodic, "I'm sure that I could *make* you do that, *if* I really wanted to..." Abigail slowly began to lower the blankets, a voice in the back of her head screamed at her to stop, but the room felt so far away, she was watching herself lower the blankets as if she was watching another person. But the idea of walking naked down the corridors suddenly felt like the greatest idea in the world. Why was she so worried about it? It was just her body after all...everyone had one... why should she feel such shame? She lowered the blankets to her chest and then, as if she was hitting a wall, her consciousness and her body collided and she stopped what she was doing. She drew back quickly, pulling the sheets back to her chin, horrified.

"Of course, it's a lot more *fun* if you do it of your own free will." The man laughed. "But if *you* like things being *taken* from you...well then...that's a whole different game..." His voice was like silk. He took a few steps towards her- she'd felt her guard lower again a few seconds ago when he spoke, but now, whatever was happening, she was ready for it, she was going to push back.

"I do not want anything *taken* from me." She spat the words out, "I want my clothes and I want to leave." He laughed again.

"I think you're lying. About both of those things."

He walked even closer and spoke in barely a whisper, "I have seen into your mind. And I know *exactly* what you want." Her eyes widened.

"What the hell are you talking about?!" She shouted, "Get out of here! Leave me alone." He chuckled as he glided towards the door, his pants tight on his legs and his shirt still wet from the thunderstorm,

"As you wish." And he left. Abigail could feel her heart pounding. Who was that man, and why was he so strange? Reading her mind? What nonsense. She'd never had indecent thoughts, and she certainly wasn't going to let some arrogant Englishman tell her what she wanted.

She settled her anger. She was still left with the conundrum of getting her clothes. Her nightdress was in tatters on the floor. She needed to get out of this room.

VII.

Resolving herself, she pulled the thinnest sheet around her and felt around…yes, everything was covered. She opened the door and scurried down the hall quickly to the room she had stayed in.

Her clothes were neatly folded on the desk. She checked around the room before pulling her skirt and blouse on. She pulled the stays on over the top and fastened it. Once dressed, she let the anxiety, anger and other confusing emotions wash over her. She sat, shaking, on the end of the bed. It was dark outside and the storm continued to rage. She had to leave. She had to get out of this castle, right now. She couldn't delay it any longer. She needed to get home, to Daniel, to her mother, even to Mr Jacobs. She prayed they would never find out about the indecent incident that had just occurred.

She pulled on her boots and cloak and ran for the door, leaving the rest of her belongings behind. She fled down the halls and staircase, rushing straight for the huge oak doors.

Once she got there she pulled at the handle, it was locked. She tugged and pulled desperately, panic filled her as she pulled with all her might -

"Madame." The old man appeared,

"I need to leave, I need to go home right now." Her voice was desperate, tears burning at her eyes.

"That is not possible."

"Please." She sobbed, pulling and tugging, "Let me out." The man shook his head gravely and the door flung open on her next tug. She slipped outside and began to run, as fast as her legs would move, the rain pelting her, slowing her, but she did not care. She had had enough and she needed to escape. She wanted an end to the peculiar happenings of the last few days and she would take whatever punishment that came with - she just needed to be home. Should she run in a straight line, perhaps she would come to the edge of the forest and be able to find her way.

Bats soared above her head, rushing past as the lightning illuminated the sky. She stumbled over the bracken and branches in the muddy groves, the castle long behind her now. Finally she could see a thinning of the trees, an edge to the woods. She raced towards it, shielding her eyes from the weather.

She looked up into the distance, at the edge of the clearing, was the castle. No…no…it couldn't be. She had run straight, she had not turned….it could not be. She turned on her heels and began to run in the opposite direction - perhaps she had accidentally come back on herself … another clearing…the castle loomed yet again. Her heart pounded in her chest. Perhaps a different direction. She ran to her left, into the thick of the trees, her feet growing sore, her heart threatening to tear through her chest under the strain of the sprint.

She could see the density thinning out and her

heart stopped as she could yet again, see the castle protruding in the skyline, the frightful beacon atop of jagged rocks. It wasn't possible. It could not be. She heard the twittering of bats and a gush of air in the wind before hearing the unnerving, English tones -

"You cannot escape. As you were told before, leaving is not possible." She turned to see the man from the bedroom standing beside her. The water dripped over his features, his clothes clinging to his sculpted chest. Abigail drew back,

"You." She snarled. He rolled his eyes dramatically.

"Yes, me." He licked his lips looking her over, "You're not making this easy. Are you?" He watched her chest rise and fall, her blood hot under her cheeks as her heart pounded.

"Why are you here? I want to go home."

"You cannot leave the castle." He looked around, "Well, you can leave the castle, *technically,* but you will always return to it." She began to run again. He kept up with ease, he was not even slightly out of breath. She ran through the thicket, the castle once again on the horizon. "Look, we can do this all night if you want to. But, just so you are aware, it does not matter which direction you run in, you will come back to the castle." Abigail shook her head defiantly. "Suit yourself." He shrugged, watching her run away. She ran forward to see him standing in front of her, waiting by the clearing. She backed away and ran away from him again, to find him again on the horizon. "You are not a fast learner." He swallowed, as if trying to suppress an urge, "Your heart is pounding. I can hear it rushing. You're going to have a heart attack if you carry on like this." He closed his eyes as if trying to remain composed, "Just give in. Go back to the castle with me. You're making this awfully…difficult." She stopped for a moment, trying desperately to control her breath. His tongue flicked over his bottom lip as he forced his eyes away from her chest and neck. She began to run again, but he grabbed her, pulling her into his chest.

She could feel him behind her, holding her steady as she pulled and pushed at him to get away. He felt so… cold. His body gave off no heat, it was like being held by a tree. His fingers were cool against her own skin - but it was cold outside. She too must feel icy. She continued to fight against him, but it was no use. He was steady and strong. She could feel the sound of his voice against her ear,

"I'm taking you back. Go warm up by the fire. It's futile to fight back." She sagged in his arms and shook her head.

"I don't want to go back there. Let me leave…" He sighed, but she could not feel his breath on her neck.

"You cannot leave." He pulled her closer. Her heart was racing. He felt oddly…secure. It was not the warm, comforting embrace she had felt from Daniel… but it was not as unpleasant as she had expected. She relaxed a little. "Come, stop this foolishness. I do not want to take drastic measures."

"Drastic measures?" Who was this man, "You're English…aren't you?" She felt him nod. Her mind raced.

"Are you a prisoner…in the castle?"

"Of sorts."

"Am I…a prisoner?" She added the words afterwards, unsure if she wanted to know the answer. He paused for a moment,

"Well, that entirely depends on what you do." The words hung in the air as he released his hold on her. She stood for a moment, the rain washing over them. Defeated, she began to march back up the crooked path towards the door.

He walked beside her in silence. For the third time, she was soaking wet and would need to change. She was angry at herself for getting into the situation again. She stormed up to the room and pulled off the wet clothing, pulling on a simple dress. She felt cold to her core and so, begrudgingly headed down to the reception room where the fireplace was lit.

VIII.

The dark haired young man was sitting in an armchair. His hair was still damp and his shirt still clung. He had his legs resting over the arm like some kind of brattish king. She glared at him as she walked over to the fireplace, warming herself.

He came over, offering her a glass of wine. She looked at it for a moment before accepting. She held it in her hands, not taking a sip. She had so many questions. There was so much she needed to know, like why she couldn't leave, even if she tried. He was the only other person she'd seen, other than the little old man. She hadn't seen the lord of the place yet.

"You said you were a prisoner here?" She asked, softly.

"Of sorts."

"What does that even mean?" Her tone was more cutting. She was fed up with the silly cryptic answers. She needed something more direct. He paused, thinking. "Can you leave, or not?"

"Yes."

"So, you are not a prisoner." She turned to face him. His arrogant face was expressionless.

"Why are you here? If you aren't a prisoner."

"I live here."

"Are you a relative of the Master?" There was a long pause.

"I *am* the master." Abigail's face faltered into confusion.

"The serving gentleman said he had served the master his whole life, are you a son?"

"No. He does not have a son." The old man must have meant he had served the family his whole life perhaps? But if the master had no son…then, who was this?

"Are you an in-law?"

"There are no in-laws. Just me."

"Right." She rolled her eyes. "So this castle, is… yours?" She was trying to wrap her head around everything.

"Correct."

"You're the master."

"Yes."

"And you live here. With the servant gentleman?"

"Indeed."

"Just you two?"

"Yes." She paused.

"You're…English?"

"Observant."

"Former prisoner?" She asked and he paused,

"Of who?" He asked carefully,

"The former master?"

"No. I am the master."

"But before you?"

"There is no before. There is only me." She

laughed.

"I'm sorry to be rude, but this castle is hundreds of years old. It must go back generations. It's clearly lived in. Who did you inherit it from?" He walked over to the armchair, sitting down again. His dark eyes watched her carefully, intrigued by her reactions to his answers.

"It was not inherited. It was gifted."

"Gifted from who?"

"The King."

"You were gifted a castle?" He nodded. "Why? You must have done something great."

"My…efforts, in the war." He steepled his fingers under his chin, a soft faraway look in his eyes.

"The war? The one happening now?"

"I have been involved in that war. But the castle and lands were a gift from a different war." Abigail thought for a moment and tried to think back through the stories her father had told her as a young girl, the country hadn't had any major wars for a long time. He was surely too young to have fought in the last one.

"Which war?" She found herself asking. Perhaps the village did not get news of every conflict.

"The conquests." His eyes narrowed as he scanned her reaction. She moved her lips slowly as she processed the information.

"The conquests? They were…two…three hundred years ago."

"Yes."

"And you're trying to tell me, *sir*, that you were gifted a *castle and lands* from your involvement in the conquests?"

"Yes."

"You surely mean your family's involvement?"

"No. I mean mine. My personal involvement." She laughed. She couldn't suppress it. Perhaps he was mistranslating and misunderstanding her...
"What do you take me for? Stop playing these games and let me have some truth. I am tired and the last few days have been taxing."

"I am telling you the truth." He came to her side. Even in the relative warmth of the castle, his body shed no warmth in her direction. She looked up at him. She hadn't realized how much taller he was, he must be easily over 6 feet. His skin was an unholy white - more so than that of the few corpses she had seen. She could not see blue veins under the sheet-white skin. Her eyes wandered over him. He couldn't be over thirty. Let alone 300. She rolled her eyes,

"What is your name?"

"Elias." He looked down at her as she accepted the information. He took another step towards her, so that their chests were almost touching. She swallowed, sticking herself to the spot. She did not want to back down. She had more to ask. She was determined that she would get to the bottom of everything. "Is there anything else you wish to know right now?" His tone was smooth and patient, his lips almost touching her own. She took a step back.

"My name is Abigail, thank you for asking."

"I know your name."

"I haven't told you that."

"You didn't need to. I know *you.* I have waited for the day you would wander into the woods. It took longer than I had hoped."

"You knew I would go there?" She shook her head. "You were there?" He nodded slowly. "You could have helped. I was lost and was trying to meet Daniel…" She closed her eyes at the thought of him.

"The stableboy? He left before you would have gotten there."

"What?" She snarled, "You're lying. You couldn't possibly know that."

"He left to go on a trade route. I showed you… don't you remember?"

"You…showed me?" She shook her head, "That was a dream…I…I don't understand…" She felt dread and trepidation set in. He placed a hand on her shoulder, it was heavy and grounding. He leant in,

"I can *show* you things. Things that are real…" He paused, a finger cupping her chin and he leant in, his lips coming closer to hers.

He was so close she could feel his smirk, and then, in a blink, Abigail was standing in the kitchen of her home, her mother talking with Mr Jacobs about the proposal. The vision vanished and faded as quickly as it had come. Elias was still impossibly close. Abigail looked around wildly as if she were going mad. His satin tones washed over her as he spoke again, "And things… that are not." The room became hazy and Abigail looked down to find herself nude, her body being kissed all over by Elias. She could feel his lips upon her skin and feel herself moaning, softly. The warmth of his hands all over her, touching her bottom...her thighs, her breasts. She could see other men and women strangers writhing on the bed, naked and tangled. They were groaning and moaning, their hands and bodies intertwined, they reached out, beckoning her to join them in their naked pile of pleasure. She felt her hand reach out to the soft black hair as Elias kissed down towards her womanhood, his warm, hot breath touching the flesh forcing her senses to tingle... The image faded briskly, leaving her red cheeked and embarrassed. She took another step back, terrified. She looked at the wine. She had not drank any.

"What...what was that?" She was shaking with terror. He smiled, coldly.

"I call them *visions.* They cannot *hurt* you." She continued to tremble. He took her jaw between his thumb and forefinger more firmly, tilting her head in the firelight. "But..." She cut him off -

"Can you hurt me?" He laughed mirthlessly at the question,

"Can I?" He snorted, "I can hurt you in more ways than you ever thought possible." His voice was still gentle and alluring. She shrunk back, "The question is... *will I?*" She gasped. Too frightened to move. Her breath shook as exhaled.

"W-Will you?" She stammered. He leant in, his lips close to her ears,

"That all depends." She could feel his cold skin against her flesh, "On if you'd like that..." She pulled back and raised a hand to slap him. He caught it, with ease and smirked at her. "Oh Abigail, that wasn't very polite." She struggled, his hand still holding hers as he pulled her closer, her face was looking up helplessly at his cocky smile.

"I want to leave."

"You cannot."

"Why?" She demanded, pulling her arm free with a sharp yank.

"Because. I have brought you here, and until I decide otherwise, you will remain here. With me." She pulled away.

"Why?" She was furious, terrified and felt cornered. She bit back, if she could never leave, then what was the point in anything? If fleeing would bring her back here, and asking was useless, then she may as well be dead. "Why would you bring me here? I had a life! I had someone who loved me and a mother to look after. I had duties and things to do. And instead you bring me here? You hold me captive? And for what? For some silly little game where you play at being king of the castle? Well I've had enough. Either make me a prisoner or let me leave. I am done with this, and I am done with you and your games." Her tone was icy and venomous. Elias's face darkened. He licked his teeth.

"Is that really what you want?" His tone was darker, edgier than before. "You want to be my prisoner? Because, *dear Abigail.* That can absolutely be arranged. I can shackle you. Keep you in a cold dungeon and end your miserable life in minutes. Is that what you want?" The words were sinister and threatening. Abigail backed away. "I saw you, running into the woods, and I knew *exactly* what you were. I saved you. I saved you from a life of misery. You just don't see it." His words crescended into a shout, "You think you were in control? You were a pawn. You would have never been satisfied in a life of mediocrity. And that's what would have happened. At best, Abigail. I could give you so much more." He drew himself up to full height. At that moment she hated him. She despised this man who thought he knew her so well.

"You do not know me. You know nothing about me."

"I know everything about you! I've been in your mind Abigail. I know everything. I know the darkest of secrets that even you do not yet know yourself."

"You're insane." She shook her head. "Do you hear yourself? Is this what happens when noblemen grow up and no one tells them *no*?" She let out a humorless laugh, "You're absolutely ridiculous."

"I was not always *noble*." He snarled. "I could take what I want from you, *whenever*, I want. I could make you *think* you were compliant." He took a step closer, grabbing her by the back of her hair, his jaw twitching and clenched, "But I haven't." He tilted his head in a moment of contemplation, he looked almost amused, "*Granted,* I had little fun with the fireplace and the battlements, but you could have fought back. You didn't. You *enjoyed* it. You *always* enjoy it." She looked away, her face burning, the grip on her hair loosening.

"That was you! I thought I was losing my mind. You made a fool out of me!" She fought to push him off. He let go, watching the rage take over her, "How dare you! What a horrible and indecent thing to make someone do. I hate you. I *detest you.*" He took a step closer, smiling,

"Oh, but here's the thing, Abigail. I really don't think you do." His voice was annoyingly smooth and convincingly certain. "In fact, I rather think you *loved* it. I saw you standing there, exposed. You could have stopped any time, you could have resisted. But no. You wanted to go further. You wanted to feel utterly possessed. I think…" He came close, whispering the words in her ear, a salacious grin crossing his face, "I think, you would have let me do the most *indecent* things to you, and you would not only indulge in it… but you would become *obsessed* with it." He pulled away, watching her carefully.

Fire lit up in her eyes. She was shaking, trembling with rage. She had so many things to say, so much poison to throw his way, it bubbled to the surface in uncontrollable, earth shattering rage, but the words would not come. And so, she screamed with anger and stormed away, throwing the wine glass into the fire. The glass shattered and the flames burst and danced. She strode away to the bed chamber, leaving Elias alone in the reception room, an enigmatic countenance across his face.

IX.

Abigail threw herself on the bed upstairs, her eyes streaming with tears. She was trapped and everything was a lie. She'd been taken over by Elias, he was the reason for all of her strange behavior. Rage burned within her. And yet...

She couldn't help the rising feeling of intrigue as she remembered how *good* she'd felt in those moments, how oddly at peace with no worries...the overarching and overbearing feeling of everything being *fine*. She steadied her sobbing and dried her eyes. Why was he doing this to her? Of course, he'd mentioned the life of mediocrity, or however he'd put it, but that couldn't be all. He was claiming to be over 300 years old, he was such a strange man. Perhaps he liked twisted games. It was undeniable that she had been unable to escape the castle - every path had led her straight back. She remembered that she had tried to run in every direction to no avail - so he clearly had *some* power. A sourcer perhaps? They were just from children's stories, surely?

She pulled herself up from the bed and pulled open the window. The storm was showing no sign of letting up and the sky was still a deep, starless black. There were no breaks in the clouds, but the glow of the moonlight could be seen daring to push through in the distance. She hated herself for getting into this mess. She'd been trapped in the village and she was trapped here. Perhaps more literally than before, but the sentiment was the same.

"It is beautiful, isn't it?" Startled, she looked around to see Elias hovering by the window. The wind was whipping his shirt, his hair blowing in the breeze, but he looked calm and collected, lounging as if on a chair in the nothingness. He folded his arms, turning nonchalantly back to the moon.

"How are you doing that?" Morbid curiosity overtook Abigail, "Are you some sort of wizard?" He laughed heartily,

"No, no, not at all. Wizards are nothing but charlatans. They do not exist." He smiled broadly and Abigail caught a glimpse of how toothy his grin was…she had never noticed before. She watched him carefully as he floated in front of her, she stumbled backwards as he delicately stepped through the window, letting himself into the room. The curtains blew dramatically behind him,

"You're…" The words caught in her throat. She could not bring herself to say them - they sounded so ridiculous. The pale skin and dark hair, the fine evening wear and dramatic castle…the saber-like canines and preference for night-time activities,

"A vampire. Yes." His eyes ran over her body, she could feel herself growing tense. She'd heard the stories of the undead, those who had sold their souls to the devil in exchange for eternal life and had curses laid upon them. She had never expected that they were real, let alone, that she would ever come across them.

"And…you're going to eat me?" She felt he was mentally undressing her as he looked at her hungrily, she felt powerless to move as he slid an arm around her waist, pulling her against him to the brink of the window. He whispered softly in her ear,

"There is more than one way to eat a lady…" He ran his fingers through her hair as he held her, brushing the hairs free from her long neck. He ran his tongue over the flesh, kissing it softly. Abigail let out a breath she did not know she was holding. She wanted to scream, to push him away, but she couldn't bring herself to do it. He was a monster. A literal literary monster, but he was undeniably attractive, and despite her fears, there was something about his presence that put her completely at ease. She'd been trying to escape it but the longer she was in his company, the more difficult it became. He was strangely addicting and oddly familiar, like the tip of senses were trying to tell her something.

She was almost motionless as he continued to kiss up her neck, before tangling his fingers into her hair, pulling her into a deep, passionate kiss.

His lips felt cold, but not like ice. He was like the cool winter chill with no breeze in the air. There was no breath in his kiss, no body heat. She could feel his tongue in her mouth, teasing her own, their lips pressed together. The cooling sensation stirred up a strange sensation in her stomach, in her loins and despite her mind fighting back, she knew that she desperately wanted more. She submitted further into the kiss, her mind searching for answers but becoming hopelessly lost in the moment, in his scent.

She reached up, wrapping her arms around his neck, pulling him closer. There was no pulse under the skin, no rise and fall of his shoulders - save his motions, he felt inanimate. It was confusingly moreish. He dragged his lips away from her, trailing down her neck once again, down to her collarbone and resting at her cleavage. His fingers moved from her hair to her breast, squeezing and massaging her. She let out a gasp, closing her eyes as his fingers slowly unfastened her stays. She found herself unresisting as he untied her blouse, her breasts falling loose from the garments. He continued to squeeze, his cold lips encasing her nipples, his tongue flicking over them. She felt them become erect not only at the chill upon them, but also the sensation. She had never allowed anyone to touch her in this way, she had never considered it would be something pleasurable to do. An intruding thought surfaced - this was surely a sin, and something only to be done between man and wife?

"This is wrong…" She whispered, acknowledging the pleasure coming from her breasts. He pulled his lips away - the room air warmer than his mouth. He continued to tease a nipple between his fingers. He spoke calmly,

"All the best things are…but this…this is not one of them" The words came between nips and licks.

"I will surely go to hell." She felt the guilt and fear well up in her, she let her head fall back, her warm fingers knotting into his lustrous hair. "This is a sin…"

"Let me take you then, be in sin with me." She placed a hand on his chest, pushing him back.

"You're the devil. You're trying to tempt me." She swallowed, trying to regain her sensibilities,

"Quite the contrary. Though, I can see you like this - you *desire* me, and I can bring you so much *pleasure.* Your god doesn't care for you. He did not care for me. Join me…Abigail, we can be together *forever* and you need not fear the afterlife…" He leant in, kissing her neck again and she felt her knees weaken.

"You cannot tempt me with pleasures of the flesh." She pushed the words out, even though she knew it to be a lie.

"Oh Abigail…" He smiled, wickedly, "I could *take* pleasures from your flesh, and when it is over, you would beg me for more, abandoning all faith in your lord and saviors in favor of the paradise that I could offer."

"You're lying."

"Am I?" The smirk spread wider across his face as he licked his lips. "I do not want to take things from you, especially as you're enjoying this so much…" His cool hand trailed up her leg and to her vagina, where his cool fingers danced. She felt a warm wetness blossoming at the icy touch. She closed her eyes. Her body leaned into him as it craved his touch, craved everything he could give her. But she could not do it. She pushed his hand away.

"No. I will not let you. I will not submit to you." He raised an eyebrow.

"If you want to do this *the hard way*, you always

were a lover of a more dangerous game…" He twisted her hair around his fingers. Brushing it free of her neck.

"I do not want your *pleasures.* And you cannot make me." He leaned in closer,

"Shall we find out?" And with that, the world around Abigail faded to black as she lost consciousness.

X.

She awoke to the gentle dripping sound of water. Her arms ached and her wrists were sore. She blinked her eyes a few times, the room coming into focus.

She was in what could only be described as a dungeon, her wrists chained in shackles above her head. Her feet could scarcely touch the floor, but her knees were still weak and without the iron on her wrists, she would fall to the floor. The room was cold. She could feel the moist air on her skin, goosebumps rising over her arms and legs. She looked down, to her complete horror, she was naked. She could not see her clothes on the floor. She scanned the room outside of her immediate vicinity. Other shackles on different walls, iron maidens and a weapons wrack. A pile of bones and stretching wrack in the middle of the room. Her heart pounded - she was surely going to die. She was shaking with terror when she noticed Elias sitting backwards on a wooden chair, looking directly at her. She spat towards him.

"Now, now...it isn't all bad." He said smoothly, "I think, when this is over, you will see things quite differently." He stood up.

"No." She shouted defiantly. "You're a monster."

"I have never pretended to be otherwise..." His

tone was silk like. He placed a cold hand on her hip bone. She wriggled to try and free herself. He grasped her hip firmly, restricting her movement, "You can struggle as much as you want. It will not stop me. Your body is going to betray you." He pushed himself closer to her, their chests touching as he took her chin in his hand, "I can hear your heart beating…you're terrified. But…" He slipped the hand from his hip between her legs, "I can also tell, that you're aroused."

She felt his fingers move over her as she tried to cross her legs, denying him entry. It was no use, his fingers were too strong. She squeezed shut her eyes as his fingers stroked the flesh, his index and pinky finger strong enough to hold her thighs apart.

"Give into it, Abigail. You're going to enjoy it. I know you are. So why fight?" His middle finger began to stroke up and down her clitorus. She had never touched herself there - the church had strong opinions on self pleasure. She felt a strange, warming sensation in her own flesh as her blood flowed to the organ, pumping it to engorgement. She bit her lip, fighting to suppress a moan. He noticed and laughed, his fingers continuing to tease, stroking back and forth in tiny, delicate motions. She could feel her legs betray her as she relaxed, her logic fading away as the pleasure began to ripple through her. "Good girl…can you feel it? Does that feel like sin to you?" She let out a moan. As she did so, his lips caught hers as he kissed her again. She felt his tongue push itself into her unresisting mouth as his finger slipped back to her entrance, sliding inside her. She gasped. His finger felt strangely large in her tight vagina. She swallowed down the pang of pain as he stroked her inner walls, caressing it gently. She could feel herself becoming lubricated, wetter with every tiny motion. She moaned more deeply into the kiss as his finger pushed deeper and deeper, to what she felt was her capacity.

"No…" She whispered, but she knew she did not mean it, she knew that she had been suppressing this desire since the moment she had laid eyes on him, but it was wrong… "Daniel…Daniel will save me…" Of course he would. He would realize she was missing and rescue her…but… her mind wandered…would he do these things to her body as her husband? The vampires lips moved to her chest, kissing and suckling at her nipple as his finger continued to dance inside her,

"I think not." He said simply, "And besides…you don't want to be rescued…not really." She was using all of her strength to argue back, but her voice was distant and dream like as the pleasure washed over her,

"You're controlling me…my mind…I don't want this. I know your tricks." He sniggered,

"On the contrary…this is all you. I can show you what my control would look like…" Without warning, Abigail felt the pleasure intensify, she twisted her wrists together and felt herself pulling her legs further apart, using all of her strength to raise her feet off the floor, wrapping her legs around Elias's waist. She leaned back, the shackles supporting her as she pushed off the floor, as he slid a second finger in. It felt incredible, magical almost. As he stretched and pulled

at her entrance, she felt white hot pleasure tear through her and she arched her hips craving more. She felt it enter her mind, the unholy craving for more. It was a possessive, obsessive pleasure, her loins aching with a heaviness she had never experienced as she felt herself grow wetter and wetter. She needed something more. Her mind was blank and awash with desire, she could think of nothing but pleasure, nothing but the beautiful stretch and the slim fingers stroking and widening her. She felt no fear or resistance, in fact, she wanted more. Her blood was hot under the surface and she could feel the emptiness, the heavy, desperate yearning for something bigger, for more force…she wanted it more than she had ever wanted anything in her life. She could feel herself about to beg, about to ask him to enter her -
He's doing this. Snap out of it. Stop. A voice in her head called out to her, but it was so hard to listen to over the ripples of ecstasy cascading over her. She rocked her hips deeper onto his fingers, writhing and wriggling like a woman possessed. She could hear her own loud moans, echoing in the cold dungeon as her wrists twisted, her legs tightening around his waist as she pulled him closer, his fingers deeper inside her as her body flooded with moisture, leaking out over his delicate fingers.

You are possessed. Tell him to stop. Don't let him win.
But it was no use- it felt too good, too moreish. The strokes became faster, fingers dancing and spreading inside her, a cold thumb against her clit - cooling the hot

and throbbing organ. She moaned and groaned, her eyes closed in an ecstasy she had never before encountered,

"Good girl. Do you feel that…how good it can feel? Call my name. Do it. Abandon all else." She gasped, her logic battling the intrusive pleasure…

"E-Eh…El…" The words were forming on her lips,

"That's it. Good girl. You are almost there. Who is your lord and master?"

"El..Eli…" Her mind felt that she was being torn in two. She could feel the mindless, beautiful pleasure but the white hot fear battling against it.

"Say my name. Abandon your God as I will give you the real pleasure you want. You remember this, don't you, my love?"

"You…you're controlling me."

"I'm impressed. You're getting stronger. I'm proud of you…" He pushed the hilt of his palm against her clit, rubbing slowly, "Can you tell me to stop?"

"S..S…" She closed her eyes as another wall of pleasure crashed into her, he grinned,

"Hm?"

"S…stop…" She gasped in breathy tones, and the red, passionate mist of calm washed away. She still had her legs wrapped around his waist, and his fingers were still buried inside her. It was a sobering rush, but the pleasure was still present. She found herself begging her own body not to respond - fighting down the urge to rock against his cooling fingers. She felt sick and horrified as the last of the mind control faded away.

"Well done…I must say. I didn't think you'd have

it in you. I like a strong woman." He licked his lips. Her breathing was unsteady, resisting his control took so much energy. He continued to stroke the inside of her gently, his wicked grin uncomfortably arrogant.

"Will you stop now?" She muttered through shuddered breaths. Elias leant in, his lip touching her ear,

"Absolutely not." His spare hand traveled up her back, over her breasts, and she felt painfully helpless, like a child's doll with no control over what would happen, a plaything for the monster before her.

"Why are you doing this?" She could feel tears burning in her eyes. He was ruining her. Ruining her for anyone that could marry her - if they even would now. She felt the shame washing over her again, her body still cruelly responsive to his touch. The worst part was that he was attractive. As much as she *hated* everything, his angular arrogant features made her heart race with excitement…but it was wrong. He was taking *everything* from her, with no regard for her feelings, no regard for what she wanted - but then - she mused hatefully - when had she ever had any control? The one time she had tried to take it, she had ended up here, in this castle, tied up in the dungeon of a vampire.

She was pulled from her distraction as a gentle finger ran over her neck. Her breathing faltered.

"I told you, I can do things to you that would make you abandon your god and call my name instead. I'm going to do that to you. You almost did it just then…" She swallowed hard. What did that even mean? He slowly pulled his fingers from within her, leaving an even cooler feeling as the moisture on her flesh clung to her in the cool air. She felt wet and vulnerable and once again, fear welled up inside her.

She watched as Elias removed his clothes slowly. His deathly pale skin was like moonlight, with blemishes and scars littered over his shoulders and chest. Taking it in fully for the first time, she saw the remnants of scars around his neck and what looked to be burn marks - fresh ones, etched in from a silver chain. She followed the chain to the ornate cross-shaped pendant. Blackened scorch marks kissed his skin where the metal was touching, it looked to be almost smoldering. How strangely bizarre. She must be delirious - she shook her head, looking away from the map of misfortune upon his skin.

His dark hair was swept back, the longer strands reaching from the crown to the nape of his neck. His eyes were dark, almost black and deep set. He looked strong, like a fighter or warrior...she supposed he was, of sorts. She wondered what efforts had earned him this castle, if that story were true, and how the scars upon his skin related to it.

She found her eyes wandering southwards to the member between his legs. She had never seen a penis before, were they all so large? Her mother had told her, of course, of what to expect when she was married... but this...this was the trunk compared to the branches she'd come to expect. It twitched as he moved closer and she felt her heart pounding in her chest.

For the first time in her life she was completely nude, with a man, who was also completely nude. She was unmarried. This was unholy, it was a sin. All of this was wrong…and yet, against her judgment she felt a pang of anticipation - the unwelcome intrusive thought of doing something she shouldn't. It felt…rebellious - or at least it would if she had any sort of say in the matter.

"I'm going to take you, Abigail." His smooth tones washed over her, "I'm going to make you my own, and once I do, you'll beg for me, over and over again and surrender yourself. You will be mine, for eternity" Conceited bastard. She spat at him. The liquid hit his face and ran down his cheek. He raised a hand to it, the saliva on his fingers. He wiped it off, no inch of anger in his expression and then sucked the saliva from the digits. He gave a lopsided smile as he dragged the wet fingers across Abigail's lips, pulling the bottom lip down. He tilted her chin towards his own face and forced a kiss upon her.

She resisted again but felt herself relax into it, his tongue once again pressing against her lips as he forced entry. He moved his hands to her thighs, pulling them roughly, forcefully around his waist. She struggled against him, it was going to happen. Panic welled up inside her, her breath hitched in her throat and every muscle, every fiber of her being tensed into rigidity.
She felt the cold head of his cock pressing at her entrance, her own involuntary moisture costing the hilt.

"This is going to hurt." His face was expressionless. "It is going to happen, regardless, and, if I were you, I'd relax and accept it. It'll be much more fun for *both* of us that way."

Abigail wriggled and writhed as she fought back tears - she could not, she would not give him the satisfaction of that. If he was to take her girlhood away, she would hold onto her dignity and her power - that was something he could not touch.

She felt him push inside her, the first inch or so - and pain seared through her. She lifted her hips trying to pull away as he violated her, but she was bound, unable to move. He held her tightly, her tense body resisting every millimeter of him. He was like ice and the feel of him forcing his way inside her was unbearable. She bit her tongue, reigning the urge to scream. He pushed in deeper and she knew she could not accommodate this. She grimaced and squeezed closed her eyes, willing for the torture to end. She dug her nails into the flesh of her own fingers so tightly that the skin began to break. She could feel the size of him stretching and bending her to him, she felt so full and tearing sensation inside of her. In her mind she prayed and waited for everything to end.

And then, it did.

He pulled out swiftly and backed away as if burnt. She dared to open her eyes a fraction to see him stood back, reeling in horror. His dark eyes had a deep red glow and they were frightfully fixated on the floor. She looked down as a couple of drops of blood dripped from her wounded vagina and pattered gently into a tiny pool on the flagstones. His eyes dragged upwards to her hands. She followed his gaze to a small stream of claret twisting down her fingers from the pressure under her nails.

He continued to back away, his chest rising and falling for the first time, his hands clawed at the chain around his neck and he squeezed at the cross. She could hear a faint sizzling sound and watched as a small amount of smoke rose between his fingers. He was shaking and was beginning to look unhinged, like he was totally insane - and then, before her eyes he appeared to both expand and contract at the same time and vanish in a plume of smoke - a single flapping bat fluttering away, up and out of the dungeon through the bars of a high window.

Abigail hung there for a moment, cold and shaking. The bleeding had stopped - it must have only been a few drops. She felt sore and stretched and beaten. Now alone, the overwhelming gravity of what had just happened hit her, and the emotions she had held back for so long began to leak out as hot tears burned down her cheek. She sobbed uncontrollably. She hated him. More than she thought possible. She cursed him and his castle and every event that had led her here. She cried until she was dry and she was sure there was no liquid left in her, and then, exhausted, and unable to move, she hung her head and tried to ignore the cold, damp air of the dungeon and prayed that fever, or death would take her,

XI.

Abigail was awoken by the flurry of rain against the walls outside. The wind was howling and whipping at the curtains. She opened her eyes weakly to look and saw a small candle burning across the room. Black smoke trailed up in twisting trails, the faint smell filling the air. Her eyes felt raw and her throat was dry. She turned over in the soft sheets, and noticed the red bruises around her wrists, and the small scabs on her fingers. She closed her eyes, blinking back tears, her breath shaking in her chest. She pulled the covers over her head and laid for a few moments in the warm darkness that enveloped her.

She tried to shut off from her senses, the bruised and wet feeling between her legs, the squeezed and scratched sensation on her wrists and the dull aching on her shoulders, the muscles sore and aching from sustaining her weight.

Her head pounded and she could sickness swelled in her throat. The horrific reality dawned on her that there was no escape.

She was trapped here with this monster. With her defiler. There was nowhere she could run, nowhere she could go where he would not find her. Her mind raced with what she could do, but all of her options amounted to nothing. Perhaps Daniel would find her. But then - how could he? Why would he? As far as he knew, she had abandoned him. He had been sent away. She had been claimed by this unholy demon, and now she would be unfit to marry. Unfit for anyone but her attacker.

She threw the sheets off and pulled the chamber pot from under the bed, vomiting violently into it. Her body trembled. She wiped her mouth with her hand and pushed the porcelain away, leant against the bed frame and hugged her knees. She rocked back and forth a few times, desperately trying to comfort herself.

There was a gentle knock at the door. She looked up as the door creaked open. The butler plodded inside and placed a small silvery tray beside the candle, bowed slightly and then left in silence. She stared at the door for a moment and then to the tray.

He'd never knocked before.

She looked around the room cautiously before using the bed to pull herself to her feet. The white underdress that she'd become so familiar with hung to her feet as she staggered over to the platter. There was a small amount of food; a handful of bread and grapes and a slice of cheese and a small goblet of water. Unsteadily, she took the water and sipped it. She took a steadying breath as she felt the water soothe her lips and throat, a little strength building in her limbs.

She felt herself begin to sob, but she had no moisture left to cry. The dry cries and wails came mournfully from her lips. She no longer knew who she was or what to think. She hated that a part of her enjoyed his company, enjoyed him taking something from her and that parts of it had felt *so good.* But he was untrustworthy. If he was like the vampires of legend, he was a cold-hearted murderous monster. She sipped at the water again, the coolness soothing her sore throat. She coughed and spluttered through the remnants of sobs and made her way to the end of the bed and perched on the end of it.

It was then that she noticed the small envelope on the nightstand. She looked at it before turning it over in her hand. A deep red wax seal with a raven and the letters 'ES' adorned it. Shakily she cracked it open and pulled the paper from inside.

The handwriting was beautiful and even, like calligraphy. It wasn't the chicken scratch she had seen in the village. This was the handwriting of monks and lawmen. Her eyes fell over the words and she sniffed, regaining her breath,

"Abigail,

You must think me a monster. Indeed, I am, but there are many things I wish you to understand. I know right now that you cannot forgive me, or believe me when I say that I know your deepest pleasures, but be assured that I do. For I have known you longer than you have known yourself. Truely, I have loved you more than life itself and I have loved you in a dozen lifetimes. I know your soul like I know myself - I know you deeply and passionately. You do not remember me, but in time, you will. You will come to love me, as I have loved you and you will see that everything I am doing is for us. For

our love. Not even death will tear us apart. I implore you to trust me, to willingly give yourself to me and let me show you my world, let me show you who we were. Submit to me and be mine once again.
I will protect you from Death himself if you will it,
Your pitiful Servent,
Elias"

She stared at the note a few seconds longer. Her fingertips brushing the ink. Anger burned up inside her. No. She threw the note aside. No. She would not submit to the fantasies of this madman. He was clearly insane, he was deluded.
She shook with rage. Looking around the room. She knew there was no escape. Perhaps she could humor him and then he would trust her…and then…then she could break free?
And if not? Then what? She looked around the room. It was a sheer drop from the window. Last time he caught her.

She looked at the bedsheet and the desk. But… what if she didn't fall the whole way? What if…

She placed a hand around her neck.

God had forbidden taking one's own life…but if she was to go to hell regardless, then, what would it matter? Her soul was already lost to heaven. She felt her fingers caress the blanket - would she dare? There would be no hope of seeing Daniel, of seeing her mother. It was a final effort for the end of a desperate, endless escape. It would be the only other way.
She looked at the screwed up ball of paper on the floor.

She reasoned with herself.

Try to befriend and escape him first. There may be a chance. Daniel would never *need* to know what happened here…

If that failed… She looked at the window.

Yes.

She nodded gravely to herself, resolving her decision.

Those were her choices.

She felt herself become steely in her resolve. Her stomach clenched as she forced any semblance of emotion and fear away. She imagined herself bottling it up, hiding it from the surface where Elias could never touch it. That would always remain her own. She swallowed and stumbled her way over to the little mirror.

She slowly combed through her hair, twisting and braiding it away from her face, allowing a few strands to fall around her cheeks. She wiped her eyes and splashed some water from the glass across her face.

She could do this.

She had to do this.

She would face her attacker and gain his trust so that she could escape. And if not..well, there was always the *other* way out.

XII.

Trying to hide the tremble in her steps. Abigail stepped out into the corridor. It was dark and poorly lit, the flamed candles scarcely lit the way.

"Madame." The voice came from behind her. Her breath hitched in her throat and she tried her best to force a smile, reminding herself of what she needed to do.

"Oh, yes. Where is Elias?" She glanced around and held her own hand, the old man's passive face suggesting no hint of emotion.

"The master is in the solar." There was a long pause. "Would you like me to request his company for you?" She thought for a moment before nodding slowly. "Would you care to wait in the great hall?" She nodded mutely again before heading down the cold stairs and along the hall into the familiar room.

She found herself studying the tapestries on the wall. One of them seemed to show a battle - she recognised the flags but some had not been in use for generations.
She looked at the two dimensional figures, marching across the image, clarions and banners in hand, helms older than her grandfather.

"It did not look like that." A soft voice came from across the room. "That hardly shows the dismemberment and sewage that covered those fields." Abigail snorted,

"I suppose you must remember it."

"I do." Elias sounded weary and his eyes looked lost for a moment.

"I suppose that it was a feast for you." She retorted sharply and she watched the pale face wince. His soft expression turned cold.

"I died in that battle." Her lip curled into a snarl.

"Clearly. You didn't die enough." Elias sucked his teeth and clenched his fists and appeared to be taking a steadying breath. She turned to face him, her eyes dark.

"You couldn't possibly understand."

"No?" She spat, "I rather think I do. I rather think *I know* exactly how it feels to die and to feel the life *drain* from you at the hands of another. To see everything wash away like it was nothing." She bit her lip. This is not what she had planned. He made her so furious. She hated him with every fiber of her being. He took a step closer to her and grabbed her by the neck, pulling her closer to him. She tried to calm her nervous shaking, looking as indignified as she could as he hissed at her,

"You think you have *suffered?* You do not even know the half of it." He dragged her by the hair to the tapestry. "Do you see that Abigail? Do you see those swords and pikes and horses? To see your kinmen torn apart and bludgeoned? And then, to be slain by a man whose face you cannot see. To lie, in the mud as hooves and armor clatter over you as the color fades from your vision?"

He pulled her to face him again. She reached up to grab his hand, trying to take some of the pressure out of his grip.

"To lie in a foreign field, thinking of your *love* back home, of the sweetheart who is carrying *your child,* that you will never meet? That god has abandoned you and so instead, you pray to someone else. You pray and you *beg*, that you will give *anything* to see them again." His face flickered in the firelight and he appeared to take a long inhale as if taking in her scent, like a wild animal about to eat. "And do you know what Abigail? Do you know why you really *don't* understand? Because someone answered my prayer. Someone *saved* me from the jaws of death, but it came with a price. It came with the most unholy and despicable of prices, and in order to see *her* again, I took it."

The last words were spoken through gritted teeth. "I *died* that day. Someone else was born. I became *thirsty.* I became *strong.* I tore men limb from limb like legs from a chicken. I feasted on their blood, and I became stronger. I took out hundreds of men. Scores. I was rewarded…" He let go of her suddenly, to gesture around, "with this. With this castle in foreign lands. For my part. For the legions that I devoured." Abigail staggered back, looking around to get away. He seemed angry now, more frightening than he ever had before. "Of course," he laughed mirthlessly, "The King did not know I was a monster. The soldiers thought me some talented night-time assassin. The savior of The English. The winner of the war. Young Elias - the baker's son, drafted in infantry against his will, the hero of the people." His eyes misted over as he looked deeply at Abigail. "Vampire, you called me. Yes. I suppose that is the modern term." He swallowed. "Do you know much about Vampires, Abigail?" His voice was becoming calmer by the second. She shook her head. "We feed on blood. Nothing else will do. No beef or chicken or pig can satisfy our hunger. It must be *human* blood. And the thirst..." He reached out and stroked her neck tenderly, "is insatiable still. I can control it for days at a time, but it only takes the smallest drop of fresh blood..." He licked his lips and closed his eyes longingly, "And it becomes an uncontrollable madness."

He smiled, but it did not reach his eyes. "We cannot walk in the daylight. That is for the *living*. And make no mistake, Abigail, I do not breathe air and my heart does not beat. The sun, created by God, scorns me. I am a creature of the night. We are difficult to kill. There are *selected* things that apparently work, but burning and swords and beheading, generally speaking, will be nothing but an inconvenience. I do not age." He reached out and touched her hair, tucking it behind her ear as he stared at her face, his expression softening again, "And, very importantly, we cannot cross water."

"But the ravine..."

"Is empty. Nothing but rocks. And bodies." He shrugged. "I cannot go home. I cannot leave for England." Abigail's heart pounded in her chest.

"Your wife?"

"Yes." His hand fell from her face and he turned away. "I realized quickly that I would not be able to cross the ses to her. And so, I sent for her. I wrote and implored her to join me in the castle. To join me here."

"And…"

"And her ship went down in the sea. It crashed and everyone on board died. I never saw her again. I died a second time that night."

Abigail felt a pang of guilt, and gently reached out to touch him.

"Do you believe in soul mates, Abigail? Lovers destined for each other?" She nodded slowly. "I did not. But then, I realized, before she died, that I could sense my wife's soul. I could reach out to her. When she died, I lost that connection. But - 20 years later I found the same soul again, wandering Europe. I implored her to me. I sent messages and beckoned her to come to me. She did."

"And…and you were together?"

"No." He shook his head bitterly. "Bandits killed her at the border. I felt her soul depart before I could get to her."

"I'm so sorry." She did not know what else to say. She suddenly felt heartbroken for the man in front of her. He was capable of such atrocities but he had also been through so much,

"Her soul returned 50 years later. I visited her village and found her, already betrothed to another man. She seemed so happy. I could not interfere. She died a few years later in childbirth. I should have stopped her. I should have pulled her away from him." He shook his head furiously. "Twelve times I have found her soul and twelve times I have lost her." He gripped

Abigail firmly by the shoulders and pulled her close to him, "I will not lose you a thirteenth time."

XIII.

Abigail could not unfix her eyes from Elias. Surely not. No. This was not true. She was Daniel's love. She knew she was. She could not form the words that spiraled in her mind.

"Every time you come back, your mind is stronger. You become less of my love than the time before. But it is you. There is only you."

"Are you sure?" Was all she could manage and with that, he pressed his lips to hers. She felt his icy cool against the burning flesh of her own mouth. She did not pull back or resist. She was taken in his arms as his hand caressed the small of her back, pulling her closer to him, deepening the kiss in ways she never thought possible. Her arms reached up and around his neck and without a thought, she was pulling him closer, his cool tongue dancing in her mouth. He tasted of nothingness, it was strange, and yet her soul felt alive, as if spring had awoken her senses and her skin prickled. Her mind felt on fire, hot with anticipation. She could feel him and see him, touch him and he felt *familiar.* She recognised the curve of his shoulder and the nape of his neck. He had felt familiar before, but was this why? Was he truly her soul mate from hundreds of years before? It couldn't be.

Lost in thought she allowed him to run his hands over her body, up and down her spine, his slender fingers brushing through her shirt. She gasped as he somehow managed to pull her closer, entwining their bodies more. She stroked away the soft hairs that brushed over his forehead, her own hands touching his neck and shoulders. She pulled away for a moment, and tried to look at his face. His features looked soft and gentle, he appeared more human than he had in days. The ethereal air about him was muted and instead he radiated safety. He opened his eyes softly and licked his lips.

In one swift movement he captured Abigail's hands and swept them above her head, walking her backwards against the wall. He pinned her against the cold stone wall and began to lick and kiss her neck with unreserved passion. She gasped slightly, closing her eyes, allowing herself to surrender to the sensation. If she was the incarnation of his wife, then surely there was no sin? Her soul was married and therefore all would be okay?

It seemed to appease her, and the inescapable sensation of familiarity continued to wash over her. She tried to search her mind for Elias's tricks - but she couldn't sense anything, this was *real*. She let herself surrender further, relaxing into his grasp as he kissed down her long, slender neck and down to her bosom.

He changed his grip to hold both of her hands together in one of his, moving his newly spared hand to her dress where he slowly began to unfasten the strings that held her breasts from view. He expertly pulled the shirt down, revealing the flesh beneath. He kissed slowly down her collar bone and to her chest, before dragging his cold tongue over her breasts and to her nipple. The nub pricked at the icy sensation, goosebumps cascading over her skin. His cool mouth encircled the nipple, his tongue flicking and dancing over it, sending jolts of pleasure through her body. Abigail moaned as she felt the tingles sparkle through her body, her loins becoming heavy and wet. She let her head rock back against the wall, the sensations washing over her. Her mind was becoming increasingly foggy in a beautiful peaceful way as she could focus on nothing but the man in front of her. She had *hated* him moments ago, she was planning to escape and run away, but now…something was different. She was seeing him in a whole new light and something inside her was desperate and longing to please him, and right now, to let him please her.

She felt Elias's hand move from cupping her breast down to her waist, pulling her hips against him. His mouth did not move and he continued to suck and lick, his tongue encircling and flicking over the tip of her nipple, his lips feeling colder by the moment against the heat of her burning flesh.

Abigail whimpered as Elias ran his hand from her waist to her hip, hitching up her dress and exposing her legs and nakedness beneath. He gathered it at her waist, giving himself access to the supple skin that was now revealed. His fingertips ran over her thighs, caressing her buttocks with the full palm of his hand, massaging the cheek roughly. She felt him grab and squeeze, eliciting more gasps and moans from her mouth, all the while his tongue continued to tease and taste her breasts. He continued to fondle her, her loins becoming hotter and wetter, in ways she never thought possible. She did not know her body could do this, could feel like this, but she loved it. Her mind felt void of all worry, of all guilt. This man had been her *husband*, in search of her for years - it was *poetic*. She surrendered further as his hands loosened their grip on her wrists and he led her slowly to the fireplace. Gently, he peeled the dress from her shoulders, allowing it to fall into a pile at her feet. He removed his own shirt with excruciating slowness before tossing it over the wooden chair. His skin was so pale, it seemed to illuminate in the firelight, the scars and old wounds decorating him like a mural. He approached her again, taking her hand in his own and pulling her softly to the ground. She could feel the fire against her skin but it did nothing to warm Elias. He laid her down slowly, took a place beside her, and then, resting one hand under his own head, used the other to walk his fingers down her naked body.

    She watched as they crept down past her chest and navel, down to the mass of hair at her groin. He walked the fingers over her thighs, pushing apart her thighs with no effort. Abigail bent one of her knees, willing him to put his fingers upon her.
Her mind flashed back to the trauma of the night before, but right now it seemed so far away, something had changed and she couldn't place it, but this felt right. It felt real and she could feel her body and soul yearning

for him.

She looked up into his black eyes, the reflection of the firelight dancing in his iris. As Elias crept his finger further up her leg and to her womanhood. Abigail closed her eyes and swallowed as his fingers slipped over her entrance, dragging the moisture up through her skin and to her clitoris. His slim fingers danced tentatively over the little organ and she felt a searing hot pleasure wipe her mind. She felt herself writhe slightly as his fingers danced in little circles, teasing and tempting the flesh. She could feel all the blood in her body rush southwards, flooding her clit, the skin throbbing under each swirl of his fingertip. She could feel the pulsing intensify as Elias continued to rub in gentle circles, occasionally dipping his fingers backwards to her opening, pulling more moisture from her. She twisted and moaned on the floor, her hips pushing towards his fingers as her vagina began to feel heavy with arousal and a long forgotten voice in her head began pleading her for a full reunion.

The torment on her clitoris continued, the frost-like fingers soothing her prickling and engorged flesh. Her fingers clawed at the rug beneath her, dust gathering under her nails as she closed her eyes in a strange ecstacy. She could feel the pulsing sensation rise from her loins and up through her stomach and into her mind with wave after wave of gentle throb washing over her again and again.

And then, it stopped. Elias pulled his fingers away slowly and dragged them to her opening. He inserted his index and middle finger, scissoring them apart to stretch the little hole.

Abigail winced, biting her lip as his fingers slipped deeper, moving apart and twisting gently inside her. She felt a moan escape her lips - this felt so different to before, so easy. Through hooded eyes she glanced up at him. He was staring down at her, drinking her in, his face a picture of longing, his eyes savoring every moment.

Abigail steadied herself with a long breath as he slid his fingers in and out, tantalizingly slow, and with each gentle touch, she became more and more ready to give herself to the man beside her.

Elias withdrew his fingers, and inserted them into his mouth, lapping up the sticky wetness. Abigail watched as his eyes flickered a deep red momentarily, before he flinched and smiled softly again.

He unfastened his pants and peeled them off, positioning himself above her, his knees between her legs. He ran his hands over her breasts and skin once more, following each curve of her waist, her hips and her stomach before leaning down and kissing her fully on the mouth again. He pulled away from the sticky kiss, looking deep into her eyes,

"I have waited 347 years for this moment, my love."

XIV.

Elias positioned the tip of his manhood at her entrance and steadily pushed himself inside.

It was cold and Abigail reached up, digging her fingers into his hair. It was painful - not as much as before, but it was not pleasurable. She squeezed her eyes shut as he maneuvered himself, the sensation strange and unfamiliar. She felt full, stretched to her capacity. She closed her eyes and gasped - the chill of his penis was somehow soothing, calming the fire inside her.

He withdrew slowly, pulling it out to the tip, leaving her feeling stretched and empty, and then, with a sleek thrust, he buried himself inside her again. She yelped out and dug her nails into the skin on his back and he repeated the process again, and again, each thrust pushing deeper and deeper than the one before.

Abigail could feel herself beginning to accommodate him, the pain was becoming less noticeable, and instead she was growing to love the full sensation, the feeling of being stretched to her capacity, their bodies entwined as one. She shakily raised her legs around his waist, pulling him in deeper.

She heard a soft grunt escape his mouth as he plowed into her again, her breasts bouncing as her body was pushed up and down on the rug, friction burning her skin. She could feel the cool air on her face and the warm glow of the fire against one side of her skin. Elias remained cold, but her own skin was becoming hot and sweaty. He felt like winter frost on a candle. The more he thrust into her, the hotter she became and the more wonderful he felt against her. She gasped and moaned, pulling him closer, feeling his skin against her stomach, her arms, her chest. Her breath hitched in her throat and escaped in higher pitched groans as he pushed into her over and over. She could feel herself throbbing, feel her blood pumping madly around her body, she was all too aware of the crescending sensation in her loins, the ever increasing pleasure and inescapable calm she was feeling.

She dug her nails deeper into his skin, scrabbling to reach for his hair and pull him even closer, even deeper into her. They were one, their souls finally reunited. She could feel something inside her building slowly, a strange fuzzy feeling in her brain. It felt as if she was soaring towards a crescendo, and then...

It happened.

A euphoric moment.

Abigail screamed his name in a burst of pleasure. She felt wave after wave wash over her, spine tingling moments of pleasure. His cool body slumped above hers, creating a heavy cool blanket for a few moments before he rolled off.

They lay there for what seemed like forever, wordlessly staring at the rafters on the ceiling, the prickle of the fire warmth still caressing Abigail's skin.

She wiped the sweat soaked strands of hair from her forehead and composed herself, sitting up slowly. She sat there for a little while, holding her knees and staring at the peacefully dancing, crackling flames in front of her. A heavy weight hung from her shoulders and she looked at them to find herself draped in a fur blanket. She pulled it around her and turned to speak to Elias, but he had left. She looked to the floor to see the stream of warm sunlight bursting through the windows. She nuzzled down into the blanket and waited until the sun had fully risen, illuminating her skin in its warm glow, before she stood up and headed back to her bed chamber, completely naked.

Once in her room she laid herself on the bed. She wasn't tired, but she didn't feel like doing anything. She was in a complete daze, feeling serene and calm, utterly content with everything.

A day before she had been panicking and angry and hurt and now...now everything was fine. She felt safe, she felt at home.

She stretched out across the bed, closing her eyes and allowing her fingers to stroke the soft sheets, taking in the soft smell of the extinguished candles and distant fire.

She didn't know how long she had laid there for, but she was awoken by a chaotic noise outside, the distant sound of rumbling and banging. She grabbed a nightgown and ran through the halls to the battlements and the windows.

She felt her heart stop in her chest.

There was a mass of people marching on the castle, and she could make out Daniel at the lead.

XCV.

Abigail's mind was a wash of confusion and horror. On the one hand, she was happy - elated even, that Daniel had come for her. He perhaps truly did love her and here he was, proving that.

On the other hand, she had just given herself to Elias - she was completely ruined. She undeniably had a connection with him - there was no way around that. Her heart pounded in her chest. She watched as dark clouds rolled in the sky overhead and the sound of thunder rumbled. Her hair whipped around her in the wind and, as she had come to expect, rain began to fall.

The sky darkened further, she had no idea what to do. She could run to Daniel, she could be free. She *should* run to him, but there was an underlying sadness at the thought of leaving the castle. A fear that she would never see Elias again and he was her *soul mate.* She was numb with emotion and confusion,

She loved Daniel.

She *had* loved Daniel. Or at least she thought she did, but those brief moments with Elias were intoxicating...invigorating. She felt a different kind of freedom, one she had not experienced before and she was craving more - craving his icy touch again and again.

She swallowed.

Perhaps, in some way, she also loved Elias.

She thought about his pale, scarred skin, his jet black hair and deep eyes. His boyish looks. He was so different to the rugged, muscular Daniel. Beautiful Daniel with his sweet soul and kind heart.

They were so different.

And right now, in this moment, she needed to choose.

Should she stay and find Elias, or run, and call out to Daniel?

Daniel was the sun - he was warm, inviting, kind and brought life. Elias was the moon. Pale and cold and dark but beautiful in another way. But - he was also a monster. He had murdered. He had killed. He needed blood. Would she ever be safe with him?

The war was still raging on though - how long could Daniel keep her safe? She didn't know. It was an impossible choice and she could not begin to know how to make it.

She felt as if her soul and her heart were tearing in two. This was not a decision she had prepared for.

Then, there was her mother. And her family duties. The need to provide. Daniel would run away with her. Perhaps she could send money back to her mother. Elias was trapped here, but the castle was large - perhaps her mother could join them?

Did she want to live forever with her mother? She felt tears well up in her eyes. She looked over the battlements to see the mob marching up the winding road to the castle. The thunder roared ferociously now and lightning bolted, illuminating the blackened sky. The rain was beginning to pour so heavily that their torches threatened to distinguish. It would be mere moments before they arrived.

Abigail ran from the battlements and into the great hall just as a booming knock echoed through the castle. In a swift, haunting blow, all of the candles were snuffed out, plunging the castle into a cold darkness. She heard the echo of the rapping on the door again and felt her blood run cold. She needed to make the choice right now.

The door burst open with a crack and a sudden hush washed over the gang as they entered. They took a few steps inside, their footsteps echoing in the hallway. Unsure of what to do, Abigail pressed her back against a pillar, daring herself to look around to see Daniel's face, and finding that she was too afraid to do so. The steps clattered deeper into the hallway and she could see the shadows cast by the firelight onto the walls.

"We know you are here, *monster.*" That was Daniel's voice. No longer soft and gentle as she had come to expect it - but rather harsh and snarling. Abigail's heart thudded. "We followed you here. We know it is where you are hiding." More footsteps, now coming up the stairs. "We know it is you that has been killing the soldiers... you cannot hide..." Other calls came from the group, and Abigail pinned herself further against the stone. He was not calling out for her

- instead he was calling out...for *Elias.* Elias had been murdering the soldiers? She came to reason with this quickly, well, he *was* a vampire after all, it shouldn't have been too much of a shock.

She waited a few more minutes, willing Daniel to call her name too, or at least enquire about her - but he did not. Bitter disappointment was beginning to creep in. She scowled, and as the footsteps came closer to the top of the stairs, she crept away, keeping her back pressed against the wall.

"I can hear you walking *monster,* do not think you can get away from us..." Abigail stopped in her tracks, her heart was beating so hard now that it threatened to burst out of her chest. Could she warn Elias somehow? She didn't even know where he was. He had vanished when the sun had come up, and it was still, though no one would know it, daylight hours. She pressed herself further into the wall, squeezing shut her eyes as she tried to work out what to do next, how to escape, how to hide.

As she peered around the corner to make a dash to the next place of safety, she felt something grip her wrist and tug her. A sharp pull and she was out in the open.

"*Got you.*" A sniveling voice proclaimed and Abigail looked up into the dark eyes of a man she had never met before. "I got the monster men, she was trying to sneak away."

A rush of feet hurried up the stairs as Abigail writhed and tried to pull away,

"I am *not* a monster." The man pulled her arm so

much she could feel the bone pull from the socket, it was still tender from the dungeon,

"We *followed* you here. You think your little *tricks* will work on us?" She tried desperately to pull her hand free as he dragged her towards the crowd amassing in the hallway. She struggled as he flung her to the ground, at the feet of the mob. She looked up into their bright torches and blazened eyes.

"Abigail?" Daniel almost recoiled, his face a picture of confusion and hurt. She pulled herself to her feet and ran towards him. He stepped back quickly and held the flame towards her, she recoiled, horrified.

"Daniel - it's me, it's Abigail, you know me. I'm not the monster. I've been trapped here for days and days and…" He shook his head, his eyes dark,

"It's been almost a year, Abigail. This is where you fled to? You were here this whole time? I thought I knew you, I -"

"You *do* know me. I got your letter, I got lost trying to find out, I ended up here. Daniel, please believe me. It can't have been more than a few weeks, I-"

"Are you a witch?" His voice was solemn. The crowd seemed to close in around her,

"What? No. You know that I am not. I've always known you, I've been trapped here, I -"

"The soldiers have been dying. We followed the monster back here. Is it your familiar?"

"Monster? What monster?"

"If she does not have a familiar - it must be her!" Someone in the crowd shouted and Abigail flung herself at Daniel again,

"Daniel, I am not a monster. I loved you, I wanted to run away with you, I was a prisoner, please believe me…"

"You don't look like a prisoner." The words were emotionless. His face had become passive and cold. Abigail backed away and shook her head.

"I was…I am…please, believe me." Daniel turned away, bowing his head.

"Kill the witch!" A voice called and the men drew closer,

"Go back to the village - her mother must be a demon too!"

"No!" Abigail shouted and reached out, but her hands were seized and bound. "Daniel please, *please* believe me." She began to sob. "I am not a witch, I am not a monster…" She was pulled about the group. They pulled at her hair, her dress, tearing it and exposing her shoulders and skin.

Over the last few weeks, she had been frightened, utterly terrified, but now nothing compared to this.

Lightning burst through the clouds again and thunder roared as they dragged her towards the door. Suddenly, the great front door slammed shut and the torches went out, leaving Abigail and the mob in complete and perfect darkness.

XVI.

The next thing Abigail heard was a series of screams and shouts. She felt cool air whip past her and she thought she could hear the fluttering of leathery wings.

She gasped as she felt her feet leave the floor and a horrible sickening sensation of movement. She shut her eyes tightly. A faint orange glow lit up her eyelids. When she dared to peek she was in a bedchamber, not her usual one, but a chamber nonetheless. It was darker in color, deep reds and blacks adorned the bed sheets and ebony posts garnished the bed frame. A few torches were fastened to the wall, flickering gently. She looked around to see Elias standing by the door, fresh scars on his chest. He glanced over at her,

"Stay here." His voice was stern and left no room for argument. Abigail looked at him, his face seemed more pointed than before, his teeth more prominent. She heard a quiet dropping sound and noticed blood dripping from his fingers. It was not his own. Before she could say anything, he popped into nothingness and a smoke filled the space in which he had been. She watched as it filtered under the barred chamber door. She looked around wildly and began to use her teeth to free her hands from the rope bonds before sagging onto the silken bedsheets.

Outside there was a cacophony of banging and screaming. The desperate shouts echoed through the halls. Abigail sat quietly, wondering what to do next.

She thought about Daniel and the shock in his eyes. That he hadn't believed her. She had thought him her lover, they were going to run away together. Was she ever truly safe with him? She felt as if she should cry again but her emotions were numb. Nothing had been as it seemed, as she expected. She had been betrayed by the very person she thought here to save her and her heart felt cold and broken.

No matter. She had Elias and even if he was the *monster*, he was mostly good and decent to her, and their souls were reunited.

She thought about him, his cold skin against her own, his pale features and dark hair. She remembered him saving her from the canyon and then again from the mob - he was also her savior. She felt a strange sense of calm in her stomach when she thought of him, she was safe here - he would protect her. From the sounds of the blood-curdling screams outside - he would *kill* for her.

She felt a strange pressure building up in her womanhood, it felt heavy and images entered her mind of his naked frame, his skin illuminated in the firelight. She felt her way up her own leg, moving her dress aside as she let her fingers walk up towards her vagina.

It was already wet, and as she began to gently touch it, she could feel the pressure, and the pleasure intensifying. She continued to rub herself gently, her fingertips dancing over her flesh, wet and warm, each touch sending tingles through her skin again and again. She felt her hairs stand on end as she circled the little bean, her fingers barely touching it.

Her back arched as she continued to touch herself, quiet moans escaping her lips. In her mind Elias was there with her, watching approvingly as she spread her legs further, continuing to explore herself more and more.

She gasped and writhed as she slid a finger inside herself, the warm cavern enveloping her. She felt around, the pressure sending waves of pleasure into her lower stomach as she gasped and moaned enjoying the sensation. She could feel her head becoming blank and fuzzy with pleasure, her fingers stroking and swirling as her other hand crept up to free her breasts from the dress. She pulled the fabric away, exposing herself to the empty room as she moaned and gasped, her second hand squeezing and massaging her own breasts whilst the first hand continued to play in the growing wetness between her legs.

She felt herself moan Elias's name, willing her to be present with her, willing that he should see her and join her, take over the control of her pleasure and indulge the fantasies in her mind.

He had been right all along - and this was where she needed to be, with him. She had given herself to him and now there was nothing to lose.

She let her eyes close and as she half opened them in the candlelight she was surrounded by shadows on the wall. The silhouette of nude men and women embracing, touching themselves and each other as they watched on at her pleasure.

She did not care. She could feel their eyes on her and it was reassuring, it was delightful. They were here for her. She continued to watch though half lidded eyes and the shadows arched and intertwined, their bodies flickering in the light. She could sense their eyes and their smiles - their moans on the edge of her hearing. She embraced it. She spread her legs wider, allowing the demonic shadows full access to her, allowing them to see everything she had to offer.

She pulled her dress completely from her skin, laying naked on the bed, her legs spread as she continued to touch herself, her womanhood and her breasts as the shadows edged closer.

She closed her eyes as she continued to feel herself, her mind peaceful and happy. The screams in the hall seemed so far away, masked by the moans and whispers of the crowd around her.

She sensed them closing in on her, their misty bodies touching her skin, brushing against her and making each hair stand on end. She could feel their strange, ghostly hands on her legs, on her arms, stroking and teasing her. She felt their fingers creep over her legs and encase her own hands, joining her in her pleasure. Abigail arched her back, moaning more and more as she felt the phantom bodies rolling against her, joining her pleasure, caressing themselves as well as her. She gasped as she felt ghost-like fingers around her neck and in her hair, her flesh reacting as if the touch was as real as her own. She could almost see their faces now. They were beautiful, like paintings. They were androgynous, all with long hair, some with breasts and some with penises but impossible in the shadows to tell what belonged to who. She didn't care. She continued to writhe in ecstasy, their fingers on her, her own fingers buried inside her, she massaged her breasts and felt the shadow hands on her nipples, pulling and teasing.

Their moans faded in and out her hearing, molding and melding with her own.

She could feel the pleasure rising, her senses heightened and intensified by the ghostly group wrapping around her in the naked pile of pleasure. She could feel the pressure and wetness in her vagina building more and more, her nerves tingling with fiery excitement.

She could feel her mind going blank in a white hot pleasure. The distant screams of those who tried to wrong her spurring her onwards as the sensations built up into a nirvana like crescendo - the phantoms arching and screaming with her as she felt the pressure flood from her body as the tension escaped in one crashing wave.

The spirits faded from the edge of her vision as she laid in a sweaty, exhausting mess on the bed sheets. She continued to lay there for a moment, panting with her eyes closed. The screams had stopped and the phantoms had completely vanished, She was alone and satisfied in the bed chamber again.

XVII.

As Abigail lay there, she was broken out of her peace by the door bursting open. She sat up, still naked, to see Elias, his clothes torn and ragged, blood dripping from his mouth and hands. The claret contrasted against his silvery skin, flowing like dark rivers from the corners of his mouth.

He staggered towards her, his eyes glowing like rubies. She stood up to walk towards him, but he grabbed her neck quickly, pushing her down onto the bed. He seemed to inhale her scent, running his nose along her neck, his eyes wild - Abigail felt almost frightened, but after the strange night she no longer had the capacity for terror. She gasped as his fingers tightened around her neck, the air escaping her lungs. He then grabbed her hip with his other hand and rolled her onto her front, as if she were weightless. He pulled her legs apart and pushed her face down into the bed.

Then, with a hand on her bottom and one still on her neck, she felt him plough into her.
She arched her back with the sensation of sudden fullness. His grip moved from her neck to her hair, pulling her head back, arching her further as he filled her again and again. She gasped and groaned as she felt

herself stretch to accommodate his fullness, her knees trembling slightly as he thrust harder and deeper into her, again and again.

His grip tight on her hair, he pushed her face further into the bed, her moans and screams muffled by the soft sheets. She could feel the slams come harder and faster, the pressure against her own stomach.

The fingers on her hips squeezed and pulled at her buttocks, pulling her cheeks apart so that she was on display to him, raw and open as he pushed into her again and again and again.

She turned her head to see the light flickering against the walls, catching glimpses of their shadows.

She could see her own, bent over, splayed, her hair pulled back. His shadow was different. It stretched and arched and moved - the shape unsettled. She could see the vague shape of him thrusting into her - however, she could see other shapes pull away from his shadow, like leaves falling from a tree. They pulled away and stretched and watched like tiny demons coming forth to witness their act.

Abigail could feel her mind losing focus - she could feel Elias's cool hands on her hot flesh, feel him filling and stretching her. She felt him possess her, *own her*, as if she were just a play thing, a commodity. She should be enraged and upset, but she could not find it in herself to feel that way. Instead, she found herself increasingly compliant, spreading herself and arching her back, pleased for his protection, pleased that the blood dripping from him was not her own.

And then she felt it. She felt the pulsing inside her.

The slight warming of his skin. It was subtle, but it was there. The steady, weak heartbeat in his throbbing member.

She gasped, closing her eyes as her own heart beat came to match it, moving herself and rocking to his rough rhythm. She whimpered as he pulled her hair back, stretching her neck as he pushed into her again, and again and again.

Then, he pushed her flat onto the bed, pulling her neck back. She felt his lips near her neck, as he placed wet, dripping kissing upon it. His cool tongue ran along her skin, blood flowing from his mouth. She felt it flow down her neck and chest, pouring over her breasts. He flipped her over again so that he could see her face.

Elias pulled Abigail's legs over his shoulders and entered her again, burying his blood soaked mouth in her neck.

Blood continued to stream over her body, a watery, sticky mess. She could feel it against her flesh, binding his skin to hers for a second, the slight pull when he moved away.

She looked up at him through hooded eyes. His own eyes were red and lust filled, his skin still pale like moonlight, shocking against his midnight hair. The scars upon his flesh now highlighted by the blood that covered him, streaming and drying up. She looked down at herself.

Her breasts bounced slightly with each thrust as he entered her. Her own skin blemished with sticky blood marks, the dried liquid clutching to her nipples, her chest bone and down her neck.

She could feel Elias growing wilder, each thrush more powerful than the last, each moan more wild and unhinged - Abigail closed her eyes and could feel herself drinking it in, enjoying how wild he was, wild he was *for her.* She let her hands wander up to his blood soaked hair, pulling him closer as she wrapped her legs around his neck, moaning and whimpering more.

The door burst open, and Daniel stood there, shirt torn and blood soaked, a wooden stake in his hands.

XVIII.

Daniel staggered towards Elias, his eyes burning with rage.

"Monster." He growled, lunging towards him. Elias pulled away quickly, disappearing and seemingly reappearing behind Daniel. Abigail crawled backwards, pulling at a sheet to cover herself.

"D-Daniel-" She stuttered, "Please, stop, it's me, it's Abigail..." He shook his head as she spoke.

"I don't know you. Abigail disappeared. You might look like her, but you're not. You're a witch." He looked her up and down, "A harlot. If you're not the witch, you're the pet of this...fiend." He grabbed her arm, pulling her upwards. Her huge eyes glared up at him, but only for a moment.

Elias darted towards Daniel, grabbing him by the neck and pulling him from the floor, before sending him across the room, clattering into a candelabra.
Daniel stood up quickly and wiped some blood from his own lip before staggering closer again. He pulled a small vial from his pocket and pulled the cork with his teeth, spitting it out into the corner. He threw the contents at Elias, a sharp sizzling sound echoing where it had caught him. Abigail watched in horror as a patch of

Elias's skin smoked and flaked. Burnt black shavings fell from his arm and to the floor, she gasped.

"Daniel, Daniel stop this *please.*" She stood up and rushed towards him, but he grabbed her arm, twisting it painfully up her back.
She could feel her own nakedness pressed against his wet clothes as he pulled her towards him.

"I loved you, Abigail. I thought we would be together. But now I see you deceived me. You tricked me with your witchy wiles." Abigail shook her head, "I came to meet you and was sent on a fool's errand where I was almost killed by the monster you live with. How many others have you sent to their doom?" He pulled her closer. She cried out in pain and Elias rushed Daniel again. Daniel was ready and threw more water towards Elias, causing him to recoil backwards in pain.

"I don't know what you're talking about..." Abigail whimpered, "I went to meet you, you weren't there..."

"Liar!" Daniel shouted, pulling her towards the door, "You will be tried for your crimes." Abigail pulled and tried to escape his grip but it was no use. He pulled her, cold and naked into the hallway. She looked helplessly to Elias who was smoking and flaking from where the water touched him. He looked both pained and enraged. As Daniel pulled Abigail into the corridor, a swift, cool breeze passed them by, and Abigail was snatched from Daniel's grip, not without pain. She shrieked as her arm twisted as she was pulled free, her vision a blur of darkness and flickering lights.

Before she knew it she was back in her chamber.

Elias picked up her nightdress and threw it at her.

"You must leave. Hurry," Abigail clambered into the dress as Elias vanished again. As Abigail tied up the front of the night gown, a flapping bat entered through the window and in a whoosh of smoke it became Elias. He was adorned again in his tight black trousers, white shirt and waistcoat, with a long black cape. He marched over to Abigail and grabbed her by the waist, pulling her close.

She could feel the tingle of his fingertips under her clothes, her skin prickling at his touch. He led her quickly to the window, and then, as the door to her chamber burst open, he jumped, pulling her with him.

Abigail felt the air rush past, the whistling sound of the wind blocking out all sound. They plummeted towards the ravine before Elias seemed to swoop mid-fall and began to ascend. Abigail gripped tightly, her hands wrapped around his neck as they climbed higher and higher, her heart pounding and racing. He soared towards the top of the castle. She looked down at the trees glinting in the rain below, the moon peeking from behind black clouds and the bottomless ravine. She felt her heart clench and she pulled herself closer to him, desperate not to fall. He gently placed her atop the battlements.

"I will take you to the edge of the forest. And then you must flee. Run as far away as you can, it doesn't matter where."

"And what about you?" She was still holding him tightly,

"It does not matter about me. I will find you

again, in this life or the next. We can never be apart."

Abigail pulled him close, breathing in his earthy, metallic scent.

"Don't leave me." She whispered.

"I will find you."

"No." She croaked, her voice breaking, "I only feel safe with you. I need to be with you forever." Elias's eyes glowed, the lightning flashed across the sky.

"Do you mean that?" She nodded slowly. "Will you be mine, for eternity?" She nodded again. His eyes glowed red and his teeth elongated. Abigail's heart raced as his lips touched her own and he dipped her into a long, passionate kiss.

He pulled away. Her eyes were still closed in the serene moment when she felt it.

The sharp pang in her neck. She felt light headed and weak, she could feel the energy leaving her and her mind fading away.

All she could see was Elias. All she wanted to do was be with him.

She wanted to serve him.

She would do *anything* he asked of her, and she would do it *willingly.*

She felt her defiance and fear melt away, sucked out of her with each lap.

He was everything.

And she would do anything.

She felt herself becoming increasingly aroused, increasingly docile and willing to do anything for him. He pulled away, blood dripping from his mouth.

"I'm…yours." She whispered, before fainting.

Abigail did not know how long it had been since the light had faded away, but when she opened her eyes, she was starving. She could hear the heartbeats of animals, of people on the edge of the forest. She felt dizzy and alert at the same time. She could feel Elias close by and the instant arousal at the thought of him nearby. She needed him, right now.

She also needed to eat. She stared at him through wide eyes, his devilish smirk.

"I'm yours." She whispered again.

"*Show me.*" He commanded. She walked slowly towards him, unashamed in the pouring rain. She pulled down his trousers and unveiled his dick. Then, lifting her skirts, she placed a hand on his shoulder. He knelt down, before sitting on the wet stones. Then, she mounted him.

She felt him deep inside her, She felt a new connection like she had never experienced before. She ground her hips into him, pulled herself up and down, moaning wildly like a fox, completely unembarrassed. She found that the more he groaned, the more aroused she became. She could feel her mind and body desperate to serve him more - and with every pleasurable noise he made, her own body became more pleased. It was as if they were one.

She needed nothing else, other than to serve him.

To do *whatever* he asked.

She rocked up and down more and more, arching her back. She felt possessed and so far away. The girl she had been hours ago, was not the woman she was now. Now, she was strong. She was his. She would spend eternity with him, with him inside her, and they would be inseparable.

She rocked more and more, moving up and down, his thick cock deep inside her. She found herself unafraid of her breasts, of his dick of their bodies. How could she have ever been so ashamed before? There was nothing more beautiful and true than this.

She bounced more. The rain soaking their bodies and washing the blood from their skin and onto the flagstones. She screamed and moaned, pushing harder and faster, her nails digging deep into his pale flesh. She could feel something building inside her, like lightning coursing through her body. Her heart didn't seem to be beating but instead she felt desperation and power.

Her head was becoming light again, her vision blurring at the edges as she rode him harder and deeper. He wrapped his arms around her waist, pulling her further down onto him, burying himself deep inside her.

They were so lost in the moment that neither heard the heartbeat or the footsteps coming up behind Elias.

Abigail threw her head back in a spasm of pleasure - as she did so, she opened her eyes just enough to see Daniel, stake raised behind Elias.

She motioned to call out.

But, she was too late.

Daniel drove the stake into Elias, from the back, the wood pushing through and reaching her own chest wall.

It did not pierce her, but Elias's eyes went cold. His face became a mask of horror as he began to smoke. He gasped for the first time.

Elias took several deep, wretched, heaving breaths before the hole in his chest opened up, the blackness spreading over his body and the skin peeling away and fluttering off into the night.

"No!" Abigail screamed, her eyes burning with tears, but it was too late. Her fingers rushed to touch his face one last time, but she could not. The last remnants of his earthly remains fluttered and danced away on the breeze - the storm fading away with him.

Abigail pulled herself up. Her eyes focussed on Daniel. He scrambled for the stake as it clattered on the floor but she kicked it away.

"Monster." She spat, and then, with a strength she did not know she had, she swiped at Daniel, slicing his face open. Blood poured from the wound as he staggered backwards. She swiped again, severing the front of his neck.

He gurgled and coughed and she watched as he trembled, falling to his knees in a shaking pool of blood. She watched as the twitching body became motionless, before bending down and dipping her fingers in the warm blood.

She placed it to her lips.

It was hot and sticky and sweet. She lapped it up and drank again, feeling her strength grow.

She stared down at the remains of Daniel and then up to the horizon where the sun began to rise. She took one final drink from his body before climbing onto the battlements to watch the sunrise.

She felt the heat on her cold skin and the painful scorch of its early morning rays. She watched in bewilderment as her skin blistered and began to peel away.

"We will be together, for eternity." She whispered, as her skin burst into flames and her world faded to black.

END

Printed in Great Britain
by Amazon